Beauty*licious

Lots of love and lipgloss smooches to:

As always, the sweet-as-sugar Anthony,
my leading man and lifetime boy crush – I heart you.

Izzy – for teaching me all I know 'bout plucking eyebrows,
applying lipgloss and how to work a room – high five!

The very gorgeous, epitome of all things Beauty*licious, Miss Sally Jones,
the King of Swanksville, Stephen Baily and the Queen of fabulousness,
Sarah Chevverchops - thanks for making my world substantially pinker just by being in it.

Vicky, Adam, Martin and Nats – I know none of you even drink,
but if you were to, you'd be really, really good at it!

The mucho talented, too-cool-for-school Laura and Jon @ Heidi Seeker
for making my world so damn pretty.

The Rains family - that includes you, Miss Chloe Rodgers - thank you
for being the best second family a girl could ask for!

And to all the feisty, fun, fearless and fabulous pink ladies who bought the
first book and who visit the website, www.pink-world.co.uk – you rock n' rule!

First published in Great Britain by HarperCollins Children's Books in 2007
HarperCollins Children's Books is a division of HarperCollinsPublishers Ltd,
77 – 85 Fulham Palace Road, Hammersmith, London, W6 8JB
The HarperCollins children's website address is www.harpercollinschildrensbooks.co.uk
The Pink World Website is at www.pink-world.co.uk
1 3 5 7 9 10 8 6 4 2
ISBN-13: 978-0-00-723534-6
ISBN-10: 0-00-723534-8
Printed and bound in China
Text © 2007 Lisa Clark
Illustrations by Holly Lloyd @ Lemonade © HarperCollins Children's Book

Beauty*licious

By **Lisa Clark**

HarperCollins *Children's Books*

Introduction

So, you want to be Beauty*licious?

Then stop dissin' your body and show yourself some love! Okay, so you may not be a cardboard cut-out of magazine perfection, but hold up, why would you want to be? You're totally YOU-nique and a chubby tummy or skinny legs are no reason not to fall head over glitter-pink flip-flops in love with yourself. In fact, it's the absolute reason why you should! So whether you're petite or curvy, tall or small, redhead or blonde, it's time to celebrate what makes you stand out from the crowd and create your own kick-ass beauty blueprint - 'coz girl, you're Beauty*licious!

#

The Beauty'licious Manifesto

Big hips, lumpy knees, pouty-lips – look, will someone please explain this whole 'beauty' thing to me? Actually, never mind – I have my own manifesto.

The Beauty*licious manifesto.
Beauty*licious is a Think Pink attitude, a fail-safe way to guarantee you feel feisty, fun, fearless and fabulous - even when your chin is threatening a major breakout. Working your Beauty*licious 'tude is all about how you express yourself - your looks, your confidence, your image, your personality – so to work it, as in like, really work it, you're going to need to:

✦ Love yourself up - get to like the person you see in the mirror - because body-bashing is just not cool.

✦ Make 'I'm Beauty*licious' your new feel-good mantra - to be repeated at least five times a day because you can never get enough sweet self-talk!

✦ Become a Beautista - know how to work and emphasise your best features for mucho bravado boosting!

✦ Don't conform - play with your appearance and have fun with your look – clash electric blue eyeliner with Brighton Rock pink painted toe-nails – colour yourself pretty!

✦ Celebrate your own unique, natural beauty – because when you're happy being who you are, you will look your absolute most Beauty*licious. Fact.

✦ Be feisty, fun, fearless and fabulous! Natch.

So banish all unpretty thoughts right now – that means absolutely no more comparisons to the just-stepped-out-of-a-salon, tall blonde girl from the cool clique, OK? Put on your pink-tinted shades and enrol at the Think Pink Academy of all things Beauty*licious!

Unlike school, we've got classes that you will love to attend - in everything from eyebrow plucking to loving the skin you're in. You'll have access to the Pink Ladies hints and tips and, most importantly, you will find everything you need to help you love, emphasise and have fun with the qualities that make you sparkle and shine like the star-girl you really are!

So indulge yourself chica, because no girl is too-cool-for-beauty school!

Academy

Your Beauty'licious Starter Kit

Pink vanity case
Pink shades
CDs
Compact
Lipgloss
Water bottle

Chica, between toi et moi, this ain't no ordinary beauty school. Nope, it's a rainbow-hued celebration of girl-fabulousness!

To maximise your Beauty*licious experience, the Pink Ladies and I have created what is quite possibly the most dee-licious starter kit in a 'so then, yet suddenly so very now' candy-coloured vanity case. It's crammed full with everything you will need in the wondrous world of Beauty*liciousness – don't say we don't spoil you!

Pink shades – how can you be Beauty*licious if you don't Think Pink? Pink Shades are most definitely a Beauty*licious Girl's most coveted accessory.

Cute compact, pink, natch. – not only a cute accessory, but also an important tool in the self-lovin' department.

Lip gloss – if nothing else, a slick of lip gloss will ensure you look like butter wouldn't melt in your pout.

Water bottle - Water is a Beauty*licious Girl's secret weapon. It flushes out the icky toxins in your body, helps your tummy to work more effectively and hydrates your skin helping to combat bad skin and spots – yay!

Beauty*licious Girl Soundtrack – feel-good tracks that will make you sing-out-loud...
Buzzcocks - Lipstick
Belle and Sebastian - Dress Up in You
Green Day - She's a Rebel
Blondie - Atomic
Beverly Knight - Gold
Ashlee Simpson - I am Me
Shampoo - Don't Call Me Babe
Cyndi Lauper - True Colours
Destiny's Child - Bootylicious

Masterclass #1
Love Yourself Up!

"I'm bee-yooo-tee-ful, baby!"

Cookie-cutter perfection is positively dullsville x 100. I mean, honestly, who wants to look like everyone else?

We all come in a range of delicious shapes, colours and sizes, each with our very own individual Beauty*licious wrapping, so instead of letting those media types or girl cliques in the playground influence your idea of what beauty actually is, make your own!

How Beauty'licious are you?

Are you a Beauty*licious babe or in need of some serious beautification?

In school photos, are you...
a. Always at the front.
b. Hiding behind the super-tall girl in your class.

If someone pays you a compliment, do you...
a. Accept it with a smile.
b. Feel uncomfortable, blush and change the subject.

It's prom time and your favourite song is playing, are you...
a. First on the dance floor.
b. Shuffling in the corner.

You're checking out your reflection in the mirror, do you...
a. Smile and blow yourself a kiss.
b. Cringe at what you see.

You're going out with your friends and can't find the t-shirt you're looking for, do you...
a. Cut and customise an old one so it's exactly what we want.
b. Ring up and say you can't make it.

Mostly a's

Sweet thing, you've got it going on!
You know you rock and you're not afraid to show it. In party snaps, you'll be in every picture and your sunny attitude will be sure to rub off on those around you. You know life is too short to worry about whether or not your bum looks big – so instead of wasting your time fretting, you shake it on the dance floor!

Mostly b's

You need a boost of Beauty*licious self-lovin'! Comparing yourself to others or worrying about people judging you will hold you back. Your real friends don't care what size is on the label of your jeans, so stop hiding. Get out there and have fun. A girl having a good time is so much more attractive than a pouty-model face any day.

Diggin' on You

When I check my reflection, I dig what I see.

That's because I'm Beauty*licious, baby!

Having a Beauty*licious 'tude doesn't mean I'm a mucho vain-girl, it just means that I'm through with hating my thighs and dissin' my chubby tummy. Instead, I love myself up – just the way I am!

If you're the put-down Polly and say things like 'I'm so fat/ugly/skinny' or 'I hate the way I look', it's not your body that's the issue, it's your 'tude.

We spend so much time trashing our bad-body-bits that we forget to love up our assets and, quite frankly chica, that's just wrong, wrong, wrong.

Negative self-talk – whether it's shout-out-loud or in your head – is toxic, so if you intend to become Beauty*licious anytime soon, dissin' yourself just isn't an option. You're a work in progress, you're still growing and changing, so why waste time bad-mouthin' your bod, when diggin' on you is so much more do-able?

What I dig most about myself is:

✮ My sugar-pink tresses that make me look like a rock girl in a too-cool guitar group.

✮ I adore my big, baby-doll eyes that would steal the screen in every scene if I were a movie starlet and how great my nails look with day-glo pink varnish on them!

✮ And I love how I laugh out loud, because laughing is very pretty y'know.

Your turn!

What do you dig most about yourself?

....
....
....
....
....
....
....
....
....
....
....
....
....
....
....
....
....
....
....
....
....
....
....

Beauty'licious Booster

If bad body talk has become a habit, break it right now with what I like to call a Beauty*licious Booster – catchy, eh?

Whenever you think something negative, like, 'I'm fat' or 'I'm ugly' stop the trash-talk in its tracks by saying something positive right back 'atcha self! With practise, your body bashin' self-critic will have to admit defeat and your self-esteem will positively sky rocket with the sweet talk, leaving you feeling allsorts of fabulous about how you look and feel.

Here's some of my favourite Beauty*licious Boosters...

"...My eyes are sparkly-gorgeous when I smile..."

"...My hair looks great today..."

"...I really know how to work a pink fishnet tights and legwarmer ensemble..."

What are your Beauty*licious Boosters going to be?

....
....
....
....
....
....
....
....
....
....
....
....
....
....
....
....
....
....

Can you feel the force?

For a whole lot of time I couldn't understand why my hair didn't come with a permanent wind-machine that made it look all swish-like and delicious. Thoughts of being a blonde-haired beauty with a buff bod used to run through my head like back-to-back episodes of The OC, and I became obsess-o-girl about getting an ab-tastic stomach and having glossy-blonde hair like the girl in my maths class. The trouble was, I just wasn't made that way. So when I realised it was never gonna happen, I got glum.

When we feel low or insecure it's super-easy to let media, peer and family pressure decide how we feel about ourselves.

It was official: I had felt the force.

Y'see, the buff blonde look that I was aspiring to, sure-as-stars wasn't my idea of beauty. It had been cleverly created by media types who have images they want us all to aspire to on constant replay - and I fell for it. Grrr.

Our bodies are going through all kinds of crazy changes like we've got zilcho control over and when we feel unsure about ourselves, it really can feel that life would be infinitely more sparkly-gorgeous if we could just fit into those skinny-fit jeans, right?

When we feel low or insecure it's super-easy to let media, peer and family pressure decide how we feel about ourselves. The thing is, when your idea of beauty is being shaped by others, it can sometimes make you feel like you're on a constant quest to become perfect-o-girl. This is pretty sucky because ideas aren't real, what with them just being ideas, and all.

But what is most definitely real, is you, so ditch the pressure to conform right now and make beauty your idea!

Snap happy

When you have a Beauty*licious 'tude you can erase other people's yawnsville ideas of beauty and perfection and replace them with your own – I know, fabulous isn't it? Think nose-twitching Samantha in the film Bewitched, except you, L'il Miss soon-to-be Beauty*licious, are capable of banishing negativity at the snap of a candy-pink, manicured finger. Who knew, huh?

This is how...

1. Stand in front of a mirror with your eyes closed and think of a compliment that someone has paid you or a situation where you have felt totally gorge-girl and confident – maybe a party where everyone told you how fabulouso you were looking or a teacher telling you that you've got an A* for a piece of work you worked really hard at. Think about it in lots of detail, what did they actually say? How did it make you feel?

2. Really think about that compliment, visualise it, make it as bright and colourful in your mind as you possibly can. Things that I think of when I'm snappin' happy are: The Pink Ladies and I watching Audrey Hepburn films back to back...Angel and I shopping for shoes...the lady who told me I looked great in my pink legwarmers and glitter pumps combo at the bus stop...having my art-girl photos displayed in a real-life proper gallery...

3. When you feel all warm and fuzzy inside, open your eyes and check out your reflection in the mirror, love yourself up sweet thing!

4. Now you're feeling all sparkly-gorgeous about yourself, snap your fingers. The finger snap action becomes an instant feel-good switch to your brain, so whenever you need a sprinkle of feel-fab glitter, just snap your fingers to activate your very own Beauty*licious confidence boost!

banishing negativity bewitched style

Bust the Myth

Shhh, you want to know a secret?

NO ONE really looks like they do in professional pics. Not even supermodels. (Cue excessive whooping and a collective sigh of relief from Pink Ladies everywhere!)

When the original mucho-gorgeous supermodel Cindy Crawford was asked how she handled the body-envy she inspired in other girls, she was brutally honest:

"WOMEN ARE ALWAYS ASKING WHY THEY DON'T LOOK LIKE ME, WHAT THEY DON'T REALISE IS THAT I DON'T LOOK LIKE ME EITHER."

It takes a whole lot of lighting, make-up, pinning, posing and airbrushing to make model-types look picture perfect. So instead of bustin' your butt trying to achieve a totally unachievable body that even a supermodel won't lay claim to, take a lesson in loving yourself up. You ARE Beauty*licious – cuddly tums, curvy thighs, bony bums included – yep, you'd better believe it!

Beauty'licious inspir-o-girls

Don't get me wrong, I still dig celeb girls. I just don't want to be them – which, let me tell you, makes my life a whole lot easier. Instead of trying to work a body shape that's just not healthy or crushing on their super-expensive matching Prada mules and handbag ensemble, I use celeb girls as a source of Beauty*licious inspiration.

In fact, j'adore my collection of 'Beauty*licious girls - past and present' mostest. They come in varying shapes and sizes and have a whole lot of totally diggable qualities, because being Beauty*licious is about so much more than looks. Fact.

Jane Mansfield – a 50's Hollywood starlet who was all curves, bottle blonde locks and lived in a Pink Palace – what's not to love?

Beyoncé – not only is she uber-talented, she will happily admit that she has to work at making her butt both Beauty*licious and bootylicious on a daily basis. Phew!

Lynda Carter – the original Wonder Woman, not only did she rock out in Lycra but she was strong in both character and physique.

Madonna – Madonna is officially the queen of re-invention, when she gets bored of the look she's currently working, well, she just changes it – my kinda girl!

Lucille Ball – the star of retro American sit-com I Love Lucy, with her famous flaming scarlet coiffure she gave red heads everywhere their very own bombshell.

Pink – not only my absolute favourite colour but also my favourite pop-girl. The embodiment of all that is feisty, fun, fearless and fabulous. Pink – I salute you!

Who are your Beauty*licious inspir-o-girls and why?

....

....

....

....

....

....

....

....

....

....

....

....

Life is sweet

Beyoncé

I rock

Madonna

Wonder Woman

I am beautiful

I heart... me!

I'm Beauty*licious

Pink

e a star!

Find your muse

Channel your inner-art-girl and create your own one-of-a-kind inspiro-art.

What you will need:
- ✦ Sweet music – to create a boho-art-girl atmosphere
- ✦ Materials with which to create - old magazines, paints, quotes you dig, colouring pens
- ✦ Scissors and a glue stick
- ✦ An Andy Warhol-esque imagination

Instructions:
Find images of your very own Beauty*licious inspir-o-girls along with some inspiring feel-good quotes and most importantly, a photo or drawing of you workin' your best Beauty*licious 'tude pose...

Now, use your material to make your very own Beauty*licious *objet d'art* for your boudoir wall. Make it as adorably delicious as you possibly can with the picture of you at the very centre, natch. When your Beauty*licious creation is finished, hang it in a prominent place, to be looked at, and adored on a daily basis.

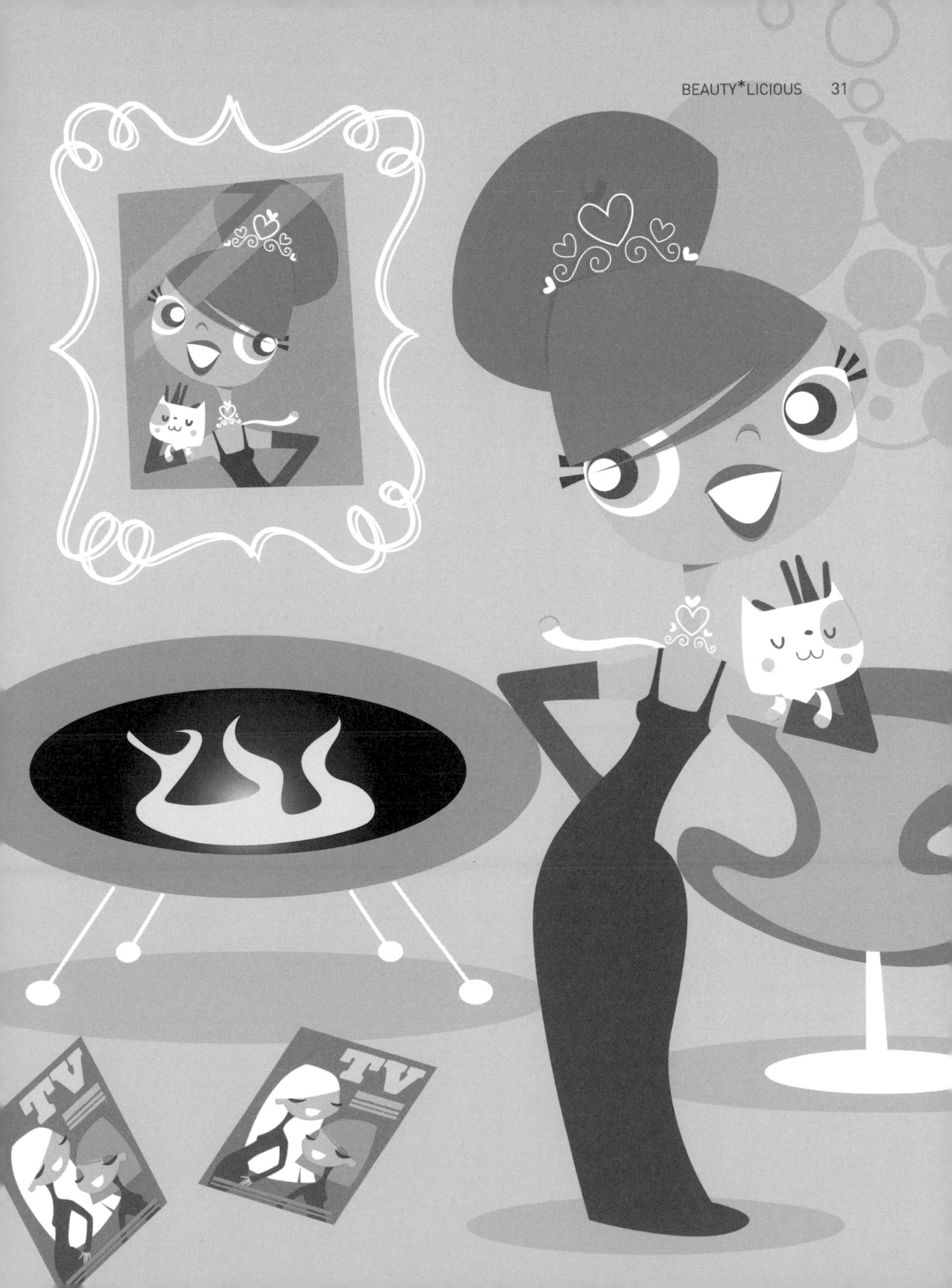
TV
TV

Under pressure

Angel: Pink Lady and all round gorgeous girl, has killer curves.

Her trunk is most definitely packing junk and she looks really rather fabulous. Yet despite her Beyoncé-esque figure, she completely bought into the whole thin fantasy.

"...IT'S TRUE, I DID. I GO TO AN ALL-GIRL, SUPER-POSH BOARDING SCHOOL IN THE MIDDLE OF NOWHERE-VILLE, WHERE THE PRESSURE TO FIT IN IS MUCHO-HIGH. THE HAIR-SWISHIN', POUTY GIRL-TYPES GOT ME TO THINKING THAT IF ONLY I WERE THINNER LOTS OF THINGS WOULD CHANGE. SO I WENT ON A DIET. A CRAZY-ASSED DIET, THAT MEANT I DIDN'T EAT, LIKE, VIRTUALLY ANYTHING.

EXCEPT, BY THE THIRD WEEK I HAD BECOME ALL SILLY AND FORGETFUL AND BY WEEK FOUR I WAS SENT HOME FROM THE SUPER-POSH BOARDING SCHOOL BECAUSE I HAD FAINTED IN THE BATHROOM. MUCHO EMBARRASSMENTO. LUCKILY FOR ME, I WAS WEARING A MATCHING PAUL FRANK UNDERWEAR COMBO AT THE TIME — COULD YOU IMAGINE IF I'D MADE A BAD CHOICE OF UNDER GARMENTAGE THAT DAY? (NOTE TO SELF: AIN'T NEVER GONNA HAPPEN SISTA, YOU'RE A FASHIONISTA!)

"WANTING TO CHANGE PART OF MY BODY WASN'T A PHYSICAL THING, IT WAS A SIGN OF MY SUPER LOW SELF-ESTEEM. I KNOW IT'S HARD TO BELIEVE, WHAT WITH ME BEING ALL SASSY AND SELF-LOVIN' NOW, BUT THE PRESSURE TO LOOK LIKE EVERYONE ELSE IN AN ALL-GIRL SCHOOL IS HUGE AND WHEN THE SO-CALLED 'NORM' IS TO LOOK LIKE A SUPER-SKINNY WAIF GIRL, THAT PRESSURE CAN BECOME ALL-CONSUMING.

"IT WASN'T UNTIL I LOVED MYSELF UP FOR BEING SO FABULOUSLY YOU-NIQUE THAT I WAS ABLE TO CHANGE MY BAD BODY 'TUDE TO A FIERCE, KICK-ASS, BEAUTY*LICIOUS 'TUDE. LETS FACE IT, WITH AN AFRO AS BIG AS MINE AND A BOOTY TO MATCH, I'D BE FOOLISH NOT TO WORK IT LIKE A 70'S DIVA, RIGHT?"

Y'see, Angel's problem didn't vanish once the weight had disappeared. Which, while rude and wrong, is an unfortunate fact. So if you're hating your bum, or not digging your thighs – even if the banish-bad-bit fairy was able to, well, banish bad bits - your life wouldn't instantly become A-list fabsville, all that would change is your clothes size.

Half the fun of growing up is waiting to find out what kind of woman you'll become and, while I know it takes a whole lot of courage to love and accept the body you've got, when you do, life is significantly more Beauty*licious, I promise! So give it a go sweet thing...love the skin you're in!

Angel felt under pressure

While Angel is now lovin' herself up hugely, if you've got a friend who isn't diggin' who she is, or feels under pressure to look a certain way, she's going to need a whole lot of girl-love from her Pink Ladies...

★ Next time she says negative things about herself like: 'My nose is too big' or 'my bum is huge' don't play along. Instead say: 'I think it's beautiful and I'm not going to get dragged into this body-bashing conversation with you.'

★ Get her to look at her whole body rather than obsessing over one part. Set aside a whole weekend for window-shopping and at-home makeovers. Anything that involves treating yourselves like the sparkle-girls that you actually are.

★ Ask her what she'd think if you were to say the kind of things she currently tells herself about you – this will help her see what a Negative Nina she's being and that trashing herself is just not cool.

Mirror, Mirror

Being you has never been cooler. You're a gorgeous dollop of sweet strawberry ice cream on a hot summer's day. Don't believe me? Just gather a bunch of your giggle girls and take a look in the mirror...

You will need:
- ☆ Yourself   ☆ Your Pink Ladies
- ☆ A full-length mirror   ☆ Paper and pen

What to do:
When we look in the mirror we usually focus on the bits we hate and ignore the rest. So, this time, without cringing, check out your reflection. Look at yourself and list five physical things you love about the chica staring back atcha – it can be the cute-as-a-button sprinkling of freckles across your nose, your incredibly long eyelashes – look at the whole person, not just one area. If you get stuck, call on your Pink Ladies for prompts – what are friends for, right?

1. ....
....
....
2. ....
....
....
3. ....
....
....
4. ....
....
....
5. ....
....
....
....

Now put the list somewhere you can see it everyday, so that if you ever feel tempted to diss a bad bit, you'll have an instant memory-jog of your ab-fab bits to love up instead!

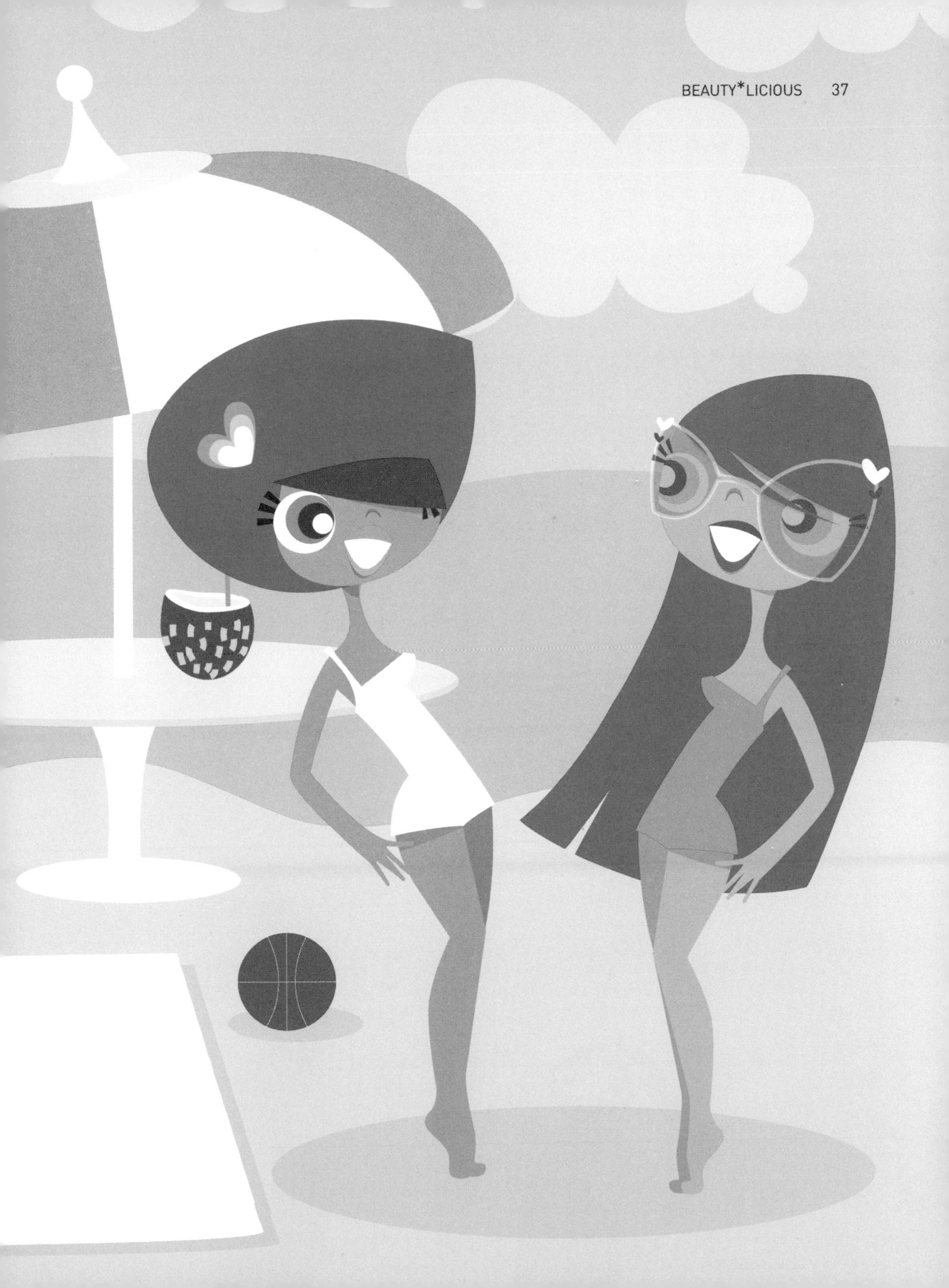

The 'Better than me, better than you' Game

A game made popular by girls worldwide.

What you need:
* ☆ The ability to diss your body
* ☆ A tape measure – to compare your measurements with others
* ☆ A speedometer – to measure how quickly you can lower your self-esteem

How to play:
It's really simple, just compare yourself to others and find fault in either them or you. Score points by triggering insecurities and lowering self-esteem. Okay, 'fess up if you're a 'better than me, better than you' game player... You might not need a game board or dice but everyone plays from time to time.

Do you measure your body against celeb-girls? Or, do you get a secret kick from knowing your legs are significantly longer than the new girl on the school netball team?

The comparison contest is by far the most popular game played by us girls. But, the funny thing is, it doesn't matter how good at it you get or how long you play for – you never win. Why? Because relying on another chica to make you feel hot-to-trot is just not cool. It's like saying 'I'm ok and you're not.' Not only will it trigger insecurities and kick your self-esteem face-first to the kerb, it will mean someone else has to appear worse than you in order for you to feel better about yourself – that's one sucky game, if you ask me. There's always going to be someone with smaller thighs, smoother skin or longer legs.

Fact.

Imagine if I compared myself to the Pink Ladies: Angel is all caramel-skin and dangerous curves; Sadie is petite, elfin-like and able to carry off too-cute ensembles that I would look quite ridiculous in: and Bella is total bleach-blonde uniqueness. I, on the other hand have pink hair and a round belly. The fact is, the Pink Ladies are all so totally different, we're just not comparable. So, instead of comparing ourselves to each other, we embrace our differences and celebrate our fabulousity because, well, we really are rather fabulous and, more importantly, so are you – just believe it, star girl!

Pretty Unique

Beauty*licious girls are quirky girls.

Yep, whether it's a brace, a cute l'il mole on your right cheek, glasses, freckles, a birth mark, pink hair, one eye that's a different colour than the other, or a gap between your front teeth - when you're Beauty*licious you work your quirks like a pair of pink diamond-encrusted Converse.

Take super-confident, fashion girl Betsey Johnson, complete with dread-locked hair tied in pretty-pink lace ribbons, an infectious energy and a talent for designing to-die-for glam-girl ensembles. She knows she doesn't need to be someone else's idea of beautiful to be a success in the world. She rocks her individuality and has complete confidence in who she is – now that's Beauty*licious!

What quirks make you Pretty Unique?

....

....

....

....

....

....

....

....

....

....

....

....

....

....

....

....

....

....

....

....

This girl will rock your world

"I'm not fat, I'm not thin, I'm me..."

Pink rocks my socks, and even if you don't love her music, you've got to give her hefty props for not following the crowd and making her very own Pink-shaped footprints in the world.

Make like Pink and instead of seeing your quirks as flaws, except and celebrate that you're Pretty Unique – because that chica, is such a good thing!
This girl will rock your world: It's not just her flashy pink hair that makes R&B/pop artist Pink stand out from the multitude of female singers fighting for a chart position; she's got a kick-ass voice, big talent, and single-handedly roasted the yawn-inducing, carbon-copy pop princesses who dominate the tabloids in her video for 'Stupid Girls'.

Pink hair and a Beauty*licious attitude.

We dig. A lot.

She says: "...I'VE BEGUN TO ACCEPT THAT LOOKING DIFFERENT ISN'T BAD. IT'S GOOD. I'M NOT FAT, I'M NOT THIN, I'M ME..."

The Beauty'licious Parlour

To avoid becoming a beauty school dropout, channel your 1950s starlet and join the Pink Ladies in the Academy of all things Beauty*licious. It's a sugar-pink parlour, complete with those decadent, squirty perfume bottles - y'know, like in the movies? This is the place to dish Beauty*licious secrets, bust myths and share advice – Bellisimo!

My friends tell me I'm not fat, but there is a group of boys who tease me and call me chubby. I want to lose weight in a healthy way. How do I do that?
THE PINK LADIES: Whoa, just because some boy-types tease you doesn't mean there's anything wrong with your body. Nobody has the right to make you feel bad about your bod, you make the decisions about you, okay? If you hang out with us a bit longer, you'll soon realise that when you're Beauty*licious, there's lots of Converse kickin' things you can do to learn to love your bod by keeping it healthy and fit!

I hate my nose and want plastic surgery for it but I know it costs thousands of pounds. I'm really sick of it what can I do?
THE PINK LADIES: Girl, surgery is a super-extreme solution and there are huge risks involved. Have you spoke to anyone about how you're feeling right now? Talking over problems with your friends, or your mum, can help put things in perspective and give you a much needed confidence boost.

Nobody has the right to make you feel bad about your bod...

I get called freckle face, it really upsets me.
THE PINK LADIES: While it might be easy to let bad-mouthed bullies get you down about your freckles, those little spots are permanent fixtures that make you totally unique. Being friends with yourself is the first step to feeling confident. So, when you look in the mirror, don't feel bad and sad about your freckles. Instead, turn them into a positive smile-worthy thing – how cute are you?

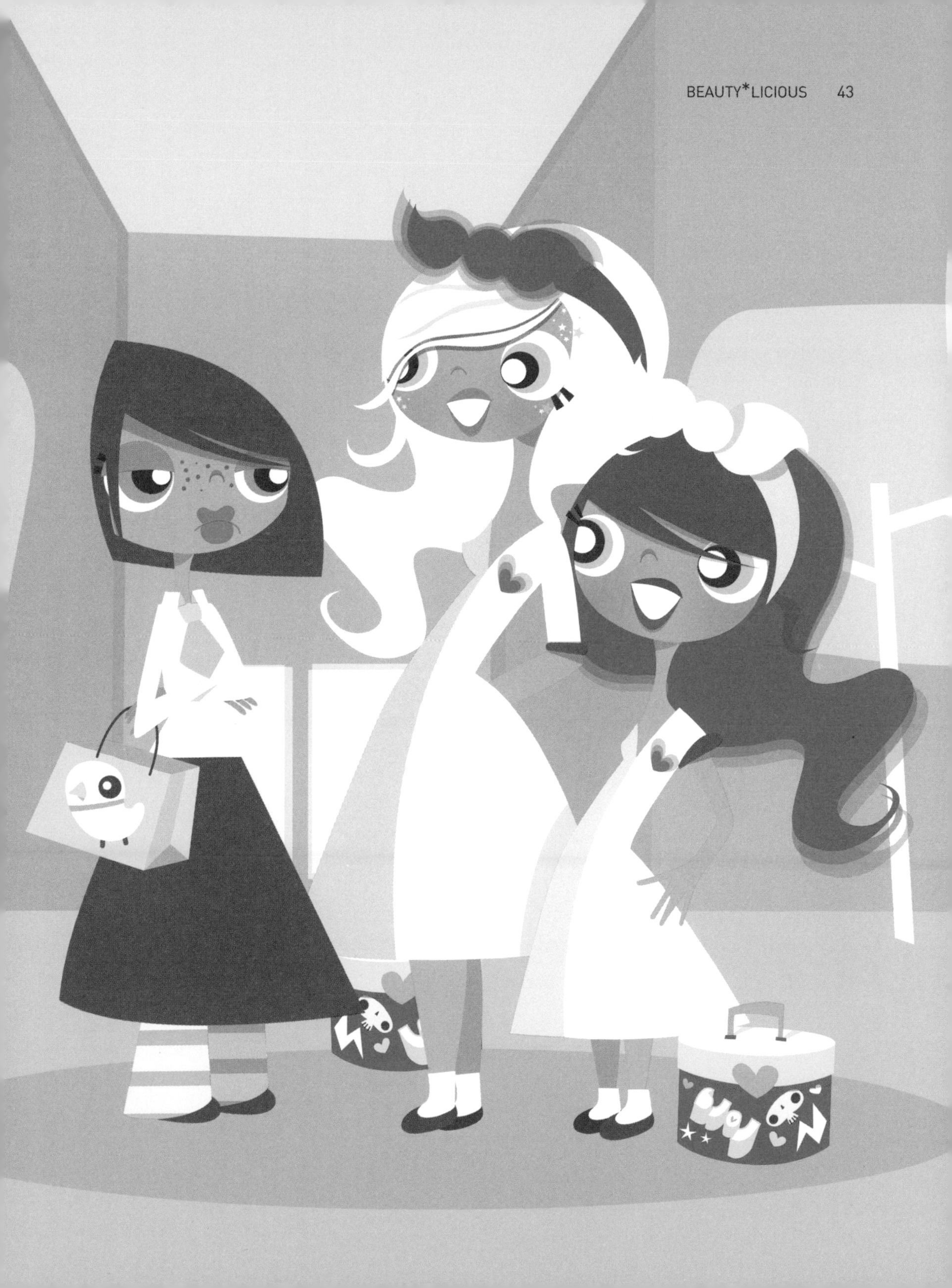

Masterclass #2
Your body rocks!

"Show your body some love!"

Body types seem to come and go and then come right back again, so it would be super-silly to become obsess-o-girl over a body shape that's likely to change, right?

Get Beauty*licious, take control and make the perfect body shape, YOU-shaped!

Are you and your body best buddies?

You're going to be hanging out together for a while, so how do you get on?

It's PE today, how do you feel?
a. All fired up, bring on the exercise!
b. Miserable x 100.

It's a Pink Ladies sleepover and someone suggests a makeover. What do you do?
a. Demand to be the model.
b. Offer to do the hair and make-up, you don't fancy spending time staring at yourself in the mirror.

You're packing for your summer holiday. What swimwear is in your case?
a. A selection of super-cute, teeny-tiny bikinis in bright colours.
b. A black swimsuit and a sarong to cover up with.

What's your idea of the perfect way to hang out?
a. Something active – like swimming or a bike ride.
b. The cinema – well, it's dark isn't it?

When flicking through the fashion pages of a magazine, what do you like most?
a. Everything – I dig trying new styles.
b. The pictures are great but I can't imagine wearing any of the outfits.

Mostly a's
You and your body are most definitely rocking to the same tune! You love your body for what it can do for you, which is why you never sit still. You take pride in the way you look and love to prettify yourself – you're Beauty*licious, baby!

Mostly b's
You're lacking serious Beauty*licious 'tude, sista! When you lack confidence in your appearance, this can sometimes hold you back. Boo. Kick-start your self-lovin' by re-evaluating how you view your body and exercise, look at activities as a way to get your body stronger and a whole lot more Beauty*licious. C'mon, I dare ya!

Angel and me getting fired up to play netball

Miss Clare
is horrible

J F
4
J B

Mr Stern sme

i woz 'ere 2007

What you waiting for?

Are you waiting to be thinner, taller, have bigger ladybumps before you really begin to live your life?

Don't.

I recently overheard a group of year 8 girls in the washrooms discussing how their lives would be dramatically different if they were able to change their body shape. As if a different body would somehow make them a different person. That made me allsorts of sad.

They were lacking serious Beauty*licious 'tude and were willing to put their own lives on hold until they fitted someone else's idea of body beautiful.

Sounds positively dull to me.

I've got far too much I want to do in my star-sprinkled life to wait until I've grown 6 inches or lost 5lbs. Being obsess-o over your so-called imperfections and how to change them sends out a super-clear message that you're not good enough. That's sucky x100. It's also not true. Check me out, I may not be everybody's idea of beautiful but I'm definitely my idea of Beauty*licious and that's all that matters, right?

Beauty'licious Body 'tude

As graduates of the Academy of All Things Beauty*licious, The Pink Ladies and I are proof that when you have respect and love for your packaging, you will sparkle and shine like an ab-fab glitter girl.

It's quite clear that we all rock very different body shapes, yet we all abide by the same Beauty*licious rules when it comes to Body 'tude...

The Beauty*licious Body 'tude Rules
* **Respect yourself** – when you give yourself respect, you make sure your body is healthy, cared for and loved on a daily basis.

* **Treat your body right** – you don't need to spend mega-bucks on your body to show it you care, just pampering yourself, eating good food and getting a good night's sleep is a really good start...

* **Don't let body hang-ups kill your confidence** – if you tell yourself that your body is ugly, your confidence will dip faster than that ride at the fairground that makes you feel a little bit sick. Both should be avoided at all costs.

* **Take care of yourself physically** – when you exercise too much, or not enough, you put your body at risk of long-term damage. Not good. The key is to choose activities you dig. When you heart what you're doing, you do it for you and not because you want to look like a pouty-model-girl. That chica, will make you truly Beauty*licious!

What would your Beauty*licious Body 'tude rules be?

....
....
....
....
....
....
....
....
....
....

Beauty'licious Butt Kicks

Kick-start your body-lovin' right now by:

✮ Smiling with confidence – smiling is a great way to turn on your body's Beauty*licious switch, even when you feel totally non-smiley. In fact, especially when you're feeling non-smiley. It gives instant feel-good factor – try it!

✮ When I used to feel grumpy and glum, I'd hide behind my mousy brown hair. Not only was it so not a good look, it sent out a huge neon-like sign to the world saying: 'do not approach Lola Love'.

So I dyed it pink.

You don't have to crack open a carton of 'Atomic Pink' vegetable dye to make an impact, just wearing your hair tied back will open up your face, making you feel and look mucho more confident and approachable – show us your face, pretty girl!

✮ No matter what the fashion-shmashion police say, don't avoid wearing bright colours. If worn on its own, black can be simply boring-snoring, so play with both your make-up bag and your wardrobe – colour is good. Fact.

✮ It's amazing how good your favourite fragrance can make you feel, so to lift your levels of lovin' - spritz yourself!

disliking my old mousy hair

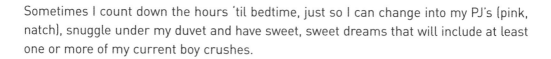

Pillow Talk

Sleeping rocks.

Sometimes I count down the hours 'til bedtime, just so I can change into my PJ's (pink, natch), snuggle under my duvet and have sweet, sweet dreams that will include at least one or more of my current boy crushes.

Sigh.

Believe it or not, an amazing, rest-filled night sleep is the most Beauty*licious body treat you can give yourself. This is allsorts of good news for me, what with me being the Queen of sleep and all. But, apparently, some people don't do sleeping at all well.

Personally, I can't think of anything worse.

How do you sleep, chica?

The 'Zzzz' Factor

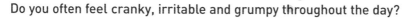

Do you often feel cranky, irritable and grumpy throughout the day?

  Yes   No

Do you snooze during quiet activities like watching a DVD or reading in class?

  Yes   No

Do you often wake up during the night?

Yes No

Does it take you more than 20 minutes to drop off to sleep at night?

  Yes   No

Do you need an alarm clock to wake you from your dreams?

  Yes   No

If you've answered yes to three or more questions, you're missing out on serious dream-time and that's just not right.

Sweet Dreams

To be truly Beauty*licious, our bodies need at least eight hours sleep each night. Could there be a more delicious way to get gorgeous than sleeping? Not in my world!

Snooze your way to sweet dreams and send those sheep packing by:

✸ Creating a sleep trigger – pick a chill-out activity like drinking a camomile tea or milky hot chocolate - mmm, having a bubble bath or reading a non-scary book and do it the same time every night. Your body will soon associate that activity with sleep and it will become an instant 'off' switch to the land of Zzzz.

✸ Shake your Beauty*licious booty - ditch all the stressy excess energy that can stop you dropping off at bed time by doing 20-30 minutes of exercise each day.

✸ Chill – banish coffee, tea or sugar after 2pm and turn your TV off at least an hour before you want to go to sleep. These are all stimulants and will make you allsorts of buzzy at bedtime. Not good.

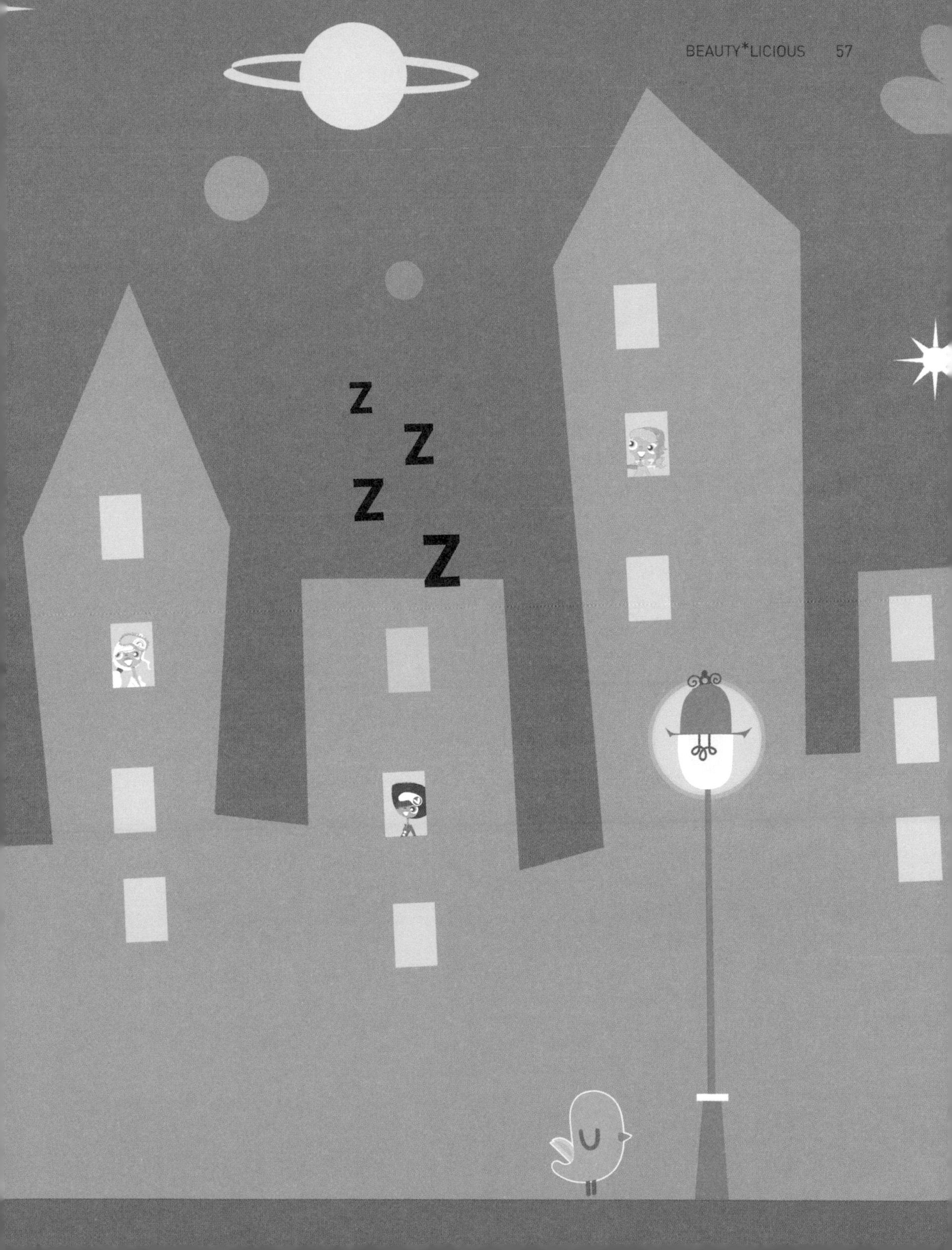
Z
Z
Z
Z

Give Good Posture

Slouching is so not a good look. Ask Bella.

"...I DIDN'T KNOW BEING SUPERMODEL TALL WAS BEAUTY*LICIOUS, ALL I KNEW WAS THAT IT MADE ME STAND OUT FROM THE CROWD AND, WHEN I WAS YOUNGER, THAT WAS SO NOT WHAT I WANTED TO DO. NOT ONE LITTLE BIT.

"I USED TO TRY AND SLOUCH DOWN AS LOW AS I COULD IN THE HOPE I WOULDN'T STAND TALL ABOVE MY FRIENDS. I WOULD HAVE DONE ANYTHING TO BE A BLEND-IN GIRL AND NOT FEEL SO... Y'KNOW, EXPOSED. BUT MY PA, WHO IS A YOGA DUDE WITH ATTITUDE, TOLD ME THAT WHEN YOU GIVE GOOD POSTURE, WHETHER YOU'RE TEN FOOT TALL OR THREE FOOT SHORT, YOU'RE TELLING THE WORLD HOW GREAT AND TOTALLY WORTHY YOU ARE.

"WHEN I BELIEVED THAT BEING TALL WAS A SPARKLY-GORGEOUS ASSET AND NOT A BORING-SNORING CHORE, I WAS ABLE TO STAND TALL — I NOW HAVE NO PROBLEM WITH GOING ON STAGE AND ROCKING OUT WITH MY GEE-TAR. I WEAR KILLER HEELS BECAUSE, WELL, JUST BECAUSE I CAN. AND NOT ONLY DO I DIG THE ATTENTION, I POSITIVELY DEMAND IT!"

Giving good posture is about much more than impressing other people, it's about putting on a Beauty*licious display of self-lovin' (even if you're bluffing and don't feel one itty-bitty bit confident). Good posture is your way of telling the world 'here I am, here's what I've got and I'm Beauty*licious, so there!'

Runway walkin'

There was no fooling the Wizard of Oz leading lady, Dorothy. She knew the Yellow Brick Road was just one long, killer runway. So, make like Dorothy and turn your own walk to school into your very own catwalk show - no slouching now!

What you will need:
- ☆ A cute boy to carry your books, because, c'mon, you're far too cool to carry your own!
- ☆ A clear path

Instructions:
To look ten-feet tall even if you're only five-foot in heels, pull your shoulders back and down - not hunched - and imagine a piece of string being pulled from the top of your head. Look straight ahead, which means no staring at your pink pumps, no matter how adorable they are, ok? And simply walk as if you're working the runway in Paris, baby!

Body Talk

Your face is by far the most expressive part of your Beauty*licious self so make a conscious effort to smile.

Our bodies can do a whole lot of talkin' without us saying a single word. How many times have you formed an opinion about someone without even speaking to them? I remember meeting Pink Lady, Bella, for the first time. She was all peroxide and snarly 'tude and I thought she was super scary. While it may seem allsorts of rude, it's a fact that a large part of the initial impression we create - some dudes in white coats estimate as much as 80% - comes from our body language.

Bella's body was most definitely talking. Her defiant posture and practised, punk-girl gnarly face was practically screaming 'don't mess with me' and if she hadn't been sitting on my bed, in my room, I would have been running in a whole different direction. Luckily, for me, it turned out that she was sweet-as-sugar under her tough-girl exterior. But her body, well, that was saying something completely different.

Make sure your body is 'talking' all things Beauty*licious by:

★ **Facing Facts** - your face is by far the most expressive part of your Beauty*licious self so make a conscious effort to smile. Your grin is a killer Beauty*licious tool, especially when you meet new people. It will help you to appear sparkly gorgeous, warm, open and friendly.

★ **Nudge, nudge, wink, wink** - Your eyes give l'il miss Sherlock-like clues to your emotions, so use them to express your interest in what's being said. When you make direct eye contact you will send a super-clear message to the person you're talking to that you're interested, calm and most of all confident.

★ **Giving good gesture** – your hands can be mucho expressive too, wave them around like an out-of-control crazy windmill and you're telling the world you're a nervy girl. Instead, use wide hand gestures to imply that you're an open and honest person and small hand gestures when you need to emphasise what you're saying.

Flaunt it!

The secret to working your Beauty*licious body 'tude is to emphasise your favourite features. Because loving your body shape is all about boosting your best bits. Now, while we all dig working our own YOU-nique style, we still need a helping hand, right?

So while those model types and star girls have super-swanky stylists, you've got us, the Pink Ladies who, let me tell you, are a totally do-able alternative!

If you're slim like Bella...

★ While I may be a wannabe rock-girl, I have slinkster hips that a rock-star boy would be proud of, so to chunk me up I wear hipster jeans with a few low slung multi-coloured belts to accessorise.

★ I wear thin layers and bright clashing colours to fill my frame.

★ My all-time fave pair of jeans are my rock-girl stretch denim pair as they help add curves to a slender figure.

★ When I'm in a 'get-girlie' mood I wear a fitted top with a swishy skirt to add volume to my lower half.

If you're sweet and petite like Sadie....

☆ I used to get grumpy about having small ladybumps, but Lola pointed me in the direction of the children's department, which is allsorts of heaven-like, and the Pink Ladies now growl-with-envy at my mucho-cheapo, cool purchases that I am able to work like a leggy model – try it!

☆ I stick to fitted clothes like tight tees and snug-fitting jeans - baggy shapes just swamp me.

☆ I wear bootcut jeans and trousers to cover my heel. It makes me look taller than I actually am, without the drama-like trauma of having to wear uncomfy heels – happy days!

☆ I've got super-skinny arms, so to draw attention to my wrists instead, I wear big, chunky bracelets – cute.

If you're tall like Angel...

★ It's easy to slouch when you're tall to avoid standing out from the crowd. I say: 'no more slouching, tall girl, you're a star-shaped princess, so act like one!'

★ If you're conscious of your height, you can break the lines with horizontal-stripe tops and chunky belts to accessorise.

★ Don't hide your legs, give your jeans a holiday and show them off, skirty-flirty girl!

★ Sometimes I have trouble getting longer leg jeans, so if they're too short I'll turn them up and wear them with my killer boots. And, yes, they have a heel – just because you're tall doesn't mean heels are banished, okay?

If you're curvy like me, Lola Love...

★ I have a sparkly-gorgeous fitted jacket that I've customised with a corsage and ribbons, the jacket streamlines my curvy figure and goes with both smart and casual outfits.

★ I've found that solid dark colours can be fabulous for curves, be sure to use scarves, jewellery and bags to add a huge hit of colour. I choose pink, natch!

★ Get measured for a bra. I used to wear a too-small bra that was mucho uncomfortable and spoilt my posture completely. A well-fitted bra keeps your ladybumps in check and gives you an instant confidence boost.

★ For a peachy bee-hind be sure to moisturise every day and don't wear too-tight undies under flimsy fabric – so not a good look.

Go For Fit!

As any Pink Lady will tell you, sport is just not my bag. Especially sport that involves catching balls – I have an inability to catch, it doesn't make me a bad person it just makes me a poor choice when playing games that involve ball catching, that's all.

If, like Pink Lady, Angel, you actually dig all things sporty then you'll know that there are allsorts of sparkly feel-good benefits to taking part in regular exercise. Angel is queen of both the netball and hockey pitch and she doesn't need a 70's revival in order to work a pair of legwarmers. She's able to do cartwheels and handstands and even the ouch-inducing splits without flinching. Angel is generally an all-singing, all dancing jock-girl.

I, however, am not.

But while I don't dig sport, I do dig exercise.

Believe it or not, keeping fit and healthy doesn't have to mean gruelling hour-long workouts or an entire morning spent on the hockey field. Just 30 minutes a day doing something to get your heart thumpin' is enough to get these feel-good Beauty*licious benefits pumpin':

- ☆ A boost in your mood
- ☆ Stressy-messy feelings banished
- ☆ The risk of icky health-related illnesses – like high blood pressure, heart disease, diabetes and obesity are reduced, phew!
- ☆ You become super flexible – go, go, go flexi girl!
- ☆ You sleep better
- ☆ You'll have mucho energy

Exercise is the easiest way to improve your health and body shape: it will help you live longer, boost your Beauty*licious 'tude and make you feel generally happier and full of energy – it also means you can eat an entire chocolate bar completely guilt-free. Now, if ever there is a reason to work my booty that is most definitely it!

Get it on!

The hardest part about taking regular exercise for me is that whole 'getting started' part and, in my experience, the first few weeks can be mucho difficult. Boo.

Don't give in though because, as crazy-assed as it may seem, once you get into working out regularly, the chances are you'll dig on it and it's always easier to find time to do things you actually dig, isn't it?

Luckily for all the slouchy couchies, you don't need an army of personal trainers to feel Beauty*licious. There are a whole lot of body-lovin' boosters that can leave you feeling fit, full of energy and fabulouso – here are some of the Pink Lady favourites...

☆ Wanna kick some ass? A black belt is so this season! Sadie and her drool-inducing big bro are real life kung fu fighters who do crazy Matrix-like manoeuvres to keep fit. High-energy martial arts help build speed, strength and stamina. Karate, judo or Tae Kwan Do are just some of the martial arts on offer.

⭐ Get your skates on – roller-skating, now that's what I'm talking about. Forget blades, I'm a retro girl, so I work my pink and cream quad skates like a wannabe pop princess working at the Hard Rock Café until she finally gets discovered. Roller-skating works your thighs, raises your heart rate and gives you the perfect excuse to wear your favourite circa 1972 outfit.

✴ Yoga – like, ohhhmmm. Bella's dad is a yoga guru, famous people pay money for him to go to their houses and do yoga with them in their fancy schmancy cribs. How cool is that? It's not just for celebs though. By combining a series of bending and stretching postures with breathing techniques, yoga not only improves flexibility, strength and muscle tone, it also helps you to chill your boots and manage a stressy, messy head. If you want to become a bendy Wendy, yoga dad recommends Hatha yoga as it's perfect for beginners. It's designed to be gentle and is suitable for people of all ages and levels of fitness.

☆ Swim to win – as well as her 84 other sporting activities, Angel hearts swimming. She even has a specially made pink swim cap to accommodate for her huge over-sized afro. Swimming is easily one of the best forms of exercise around as it promotes strength, stamina and mobility, resulting in all-round feel-good fitness.

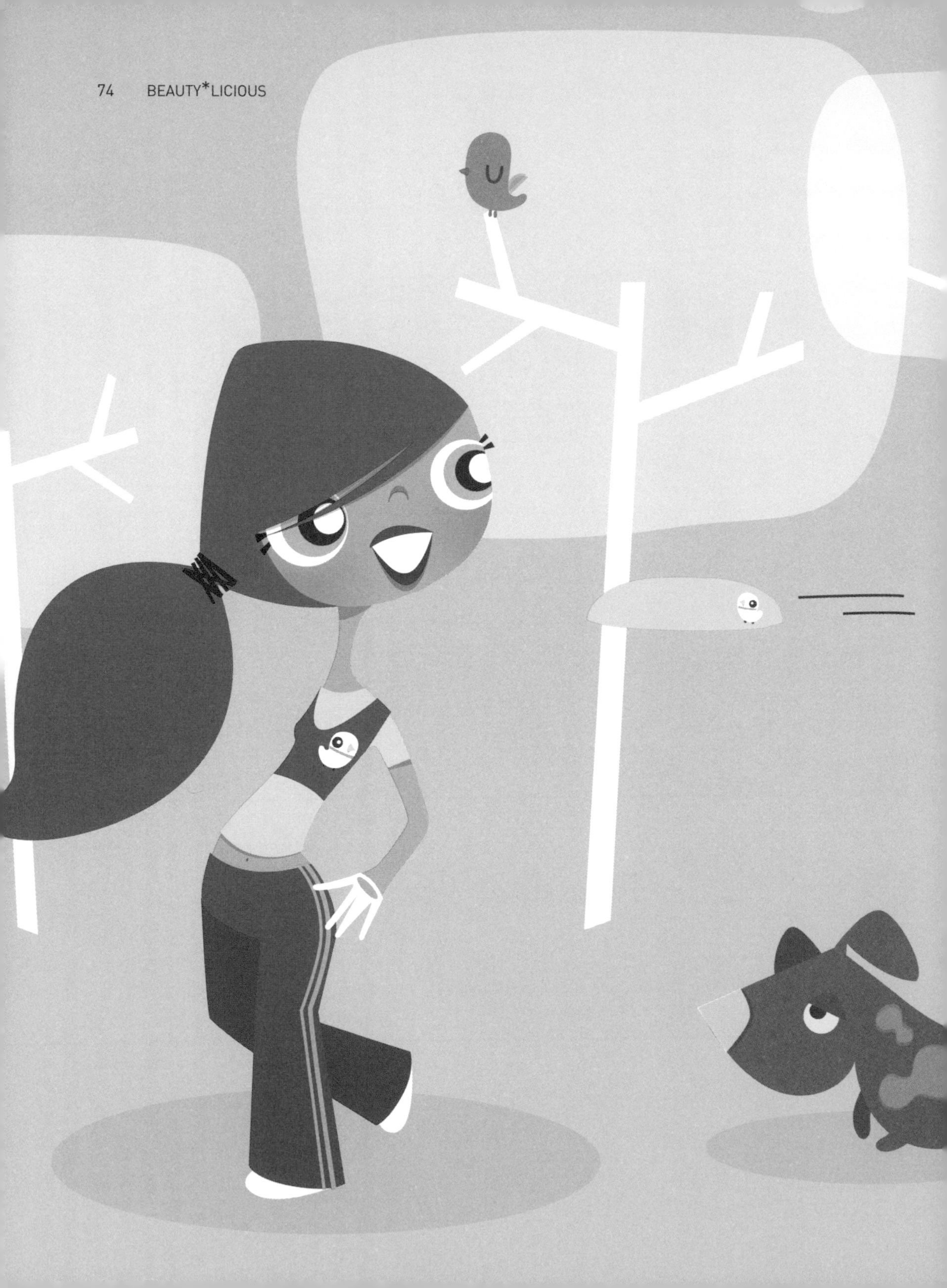

So, what's your excuse?

Slouchy couchies are the best excuse makers. I should know, I used to be one. Whatever excuse you make to get yourself out of exercise, I can guarantee that Pink Lady, Angel, will have a response. She's ever-so annoying like that.

You'd love to exercise but you don't have any free time?

Being a modern girl means being a busy girl, but exercise doesn't have to be time consuming:

☆ Grab some baked bean tins, (full ones, of course!) and do bicep curls as you watch TV.

☆ Earn extra money, win over the parentals and get fit by opting to do chores that will keep you active, like cleaning windows or hoovering.

☆ Don't just stand on the escalator at the shopping centre, walk up it, lazy Mazie!

You want to get fit but you're too young/too self-conscious to join a gym? You don't have to join a gym to get fit:

☆ Grab your Pink Ladies and head to the park for free Frisbee throwing.

☆ Work it on the dance floor, Beyonce style. Haven't got a dance floor? Clear some space on your bedroom carpet and crank up your favourite tune.

☆ If you're not completely adverse to sport, join a school sports team - you'll get fit and make friends at the same time.

On your marks, get set, GO!

Before you throw yourself into a hazy crazy get-fit regime you're never going to stick to – start by letting your body know your new Beauty*licious lifestyle starts right here, right now, by:

✯ **Making an appointment with yourself –** at the beginning of each week, write your sessions in your diary, just like you would a haircut, a friend's birthday or a soiree. Treat getting fit like any other date and be sure to stick to it!

✯ **Ask your Pink Ladies to be cheerleaders** – enlist their help to kick your bee-hind with 'go-girl' phone calls, texts and email reminders to work out.

✯ **Make it fun –** because you'll never fall in love with exercise if you hate what you're doing. Try everything from yoga to aerobics until you find something you enjoy. Try something you've never done before, dare ya!

✯ **Reward yourself –** so you've stuck at your chosen activity for a whole two weeks? Well done you! Treat yourself to an O.C.-DVD-athon, some cute-as-a-button workout pumps, or a day of pampering. When you treat yourself you're much more likely to keep up your activity!

my own cheerleaders!

L'il Miss Motivator!

If you find the whole process of doing physical activity semi-traumatic and throw a drama-laden hissyfit at the mere mention of the word 'exercise' - you're gonna need to become L'il Miss Motivator. Tight-fitting Lycra is, as always, optional.

I have my own L'il Miss Motivator, jock-girl Angel.

Lucky me.

But she's not here all year round, so in order to keep fit I have to create my own bee-hind kickers, feel free to borrow them!

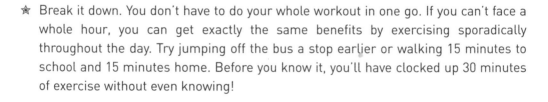

★ Break it down. You don't have to do your whole workout in one go. If you can't face a whole hour, you can get exactly the same benefits by exercising sporadically throughout the day. Try jumping off the bus a stop earlier or walking 15 minutes to school and 15 minutes home. Before you know it, you'll have clocked up 30 minutes of exercise without even knowing!

★ If you're a regular slouchy-couchy, start with something easy such as Speedy Girl walks – a short SG walk will give your heart, lungs and leg muscles a good workout. Start by walking for 5-10 minutes a day and build this up adding 2-3 minutes each time.

★ Celebrate the benefits - along with being l'il miss energy, you will start feeling less stressy and generally much more happier. So when you notice improvements, register them, write them down and celebrate 'em, chica!

★ This baby is guaranteed to get results - get yourself some super cute exercise clothes. Changing into them, even when you don't feel like working out, raises the chances of you actually going ahead and breaking into a sweat – seeing as how you're dressed for it and all!

Work it, girl!

Okay, so you're not mad about getting Sweaty-Betty in public, why not make like the Pink Ladies and get your rock on in the comfort of your own boudoir?

BTW: We are more than cool with you stealing our moves.

What you will need:
* Floor space
* Three tunes from your favourite musical moment in time
* The ability to channel your favourite 'era icon'

Instructions:
Forget super choreographed shape throwin', this is all about bustin' some killer era-inspired moves for fun!
1. Pencil three 'work it, girl!' sessions in your diary for the next week
2. Feel free to accessorise your comfy ensemble with era-related items
3. Before you continue, channel an era icon of your choice to maximise the experience
4. Now, shake your booty to warm yourself up, pop the CD in the slot and press play, sweet thing!

The Pink Ladies all do at least three 'work it, girl!' sessions a week, so to make sure we never get bored, we swap mix CDs and work a different era each time we exercise – coolio, eh? Maybe you and your Pink Ladies could do the same...

In the meantime, try out Bella and Sadie's most recent 'work it, girl!' sessions – who knew exercise could be this fun?

Bella's rock-girl workout

Sample tunes:
The Clash – London Calling
Green Day - She's a Rebel
The Ramones – Let's Dance

Channel:
The skinny-hipped, Joey Ramone. Sigh.

Bella's favourite era-inspired move

The Air Guitar

1. Stand with feet apart, turn left foot out at an angle and bend knee slightly. Keep right leg straight. Bring your left arm straight out to your side with your hand in a fist.

2. The next two steps should be done in a fluid motion. Swing your right arm forward in a circular motion; it should meet your left arm and continue round to make a circle. As you do this with your arms, kick your right leg across your left at an angle so it's even with your left arm.

3. Bend and lift your right knee until your heel lines up with your left knee and jump up and down on your left leg. Keep swinging your arm in a circle like you're a rock star thrashing her guitar! Repeat on the right – right leg bent, right arm out to the side. Do this for one minute each side to the beat of the music.

Rock out!

Sadie's Dancing Queen routine

Sample tunes:
Abba – Dancing Queen, natch.
KC & the Sunshine Band – (shake, shake, shake) Shake your booty
The Bee Gees – Night Fever

Channel:
Benny and Bjorn complete with white spandex jumpsuits and a whole lot of hair.

Sadie's favourite era-inspired moves

The Pivot turn
Keeping your left foot on the spot, use your right foot to move your body round in a circle towards the left. Take three steps to twist round 'til you're facing forward again. Repeat x 5.

The Tap
Step to the left with your left foot. Follow with your right, tapping it down next to the left. Clap twice in time to the music. Repeat to the right.

The Grapevine
1. Step to the right and take your left foot behind, bending your right arm at the elbow. Bring your left arm to meet your right and clap.

2. step to the right, follow with the left foot (feet together). The move goes: wide step, cross feet behind, wide step, feet together. Repeat on the other side.

Watch that scene, chica, you're the dancing queen!

Your 'Work it Girl!' Routine

What era do you dig?

....
....
....
....
....
....

What tunes will you put on your mix cd?

....
....
....
....
....
....
....
....

What era-icon will you channel?

....
....
....
....
....
....
....

What's your favourite era-related move?

....
....
....
....
....

The Pink Ladies 'work it, girl' tips

☆ Always warm up and cool down with gentle stretches – this way you won't pull any muscles.

☆ If you feel any pain during exercise, stop!

☆ Drink water before, during and after a workout.

☆ If you're poorly-sick don't exercise – it'll only make you worse.

☆ It's important not to get super obsess-o with exercise; we all need a healthy balance.

day	am	pm
MONDAY...............		
TUESDAY...............		
WEDNESDAY..............		
THURSDAY...........		
FRIDAY...........		
SATURDAY...........		
SUNDAY...........		

Result!

Stick to your own customised Beauty*licious plan of 30 minutes body-pumpin' of your choice and you'll soon start seeing the benefits...

2 weeks - you'll feel happier. When you exercise mood bustin' chemicals called endorphins are released.

4 weeks - you'll have more energy. All the exercise will help you sleep better and steady your energy levels.

6 weeks - you'll swap fat for muscle. This means more tone and less wobble – yay!

3 months - you'll have boosted your confidence. Your body will work better and look better and that will make you feel better.

6 months - exercise will be a habit and together with healthy eating will boost your memory and powers of concentration.

Go – for – it girl!

The Beauty'licous Parlour

Come inside, body rockers...

I'm totally bored with exercise. Any ideas?

THE PINK LADIES: If our 'Work It, Girl' routines aren't enough to get your body movin' and groovin' then how about the bhangra workout? Available at masaladance.com it incorporates popular dance moves from India into one shoulder- bobbing, hip-swivelling aerobic frenzy. Don't get the idea that this is any less intense than the feel-the-burn videos gathering dust next to our dumbbells. We are already five-kinds of sore after test driving the DVD, plus you don't have to deal with some dizzy chick telling you that you're 'doing awe-some'!

I'd really like to try Ballet, but do I need to be super fit already?

THE PINK LADIES: Ballet is a fantastic form of exercise and will improve your posture dramatically. You'll become fitter as the classes go on and it'll be exciting to see how your body reacts. Go for it!

When is it best to exercise – morning, afternoon or night?

THE PINK LADIES: The best time to get movin' is when you're feeling it. We all tend to have a point in the afternoon when hormone levels change. Figure out if you like to work out before, after or during that energy lull. Some feel more awake if they exercise in the am, others like to give themselves a jolt in the pm. Many don't have time to exercise until the evening. Simply choose the time you feel most energetic so you stick to your routine.

I'm a slouchy couchy – what can I do to ease me into exercise?

THE PINK LADIES: How about Hula-hooping? This retro throwback activity is by far the coolest way to get fit and is so much fun you won't even feel like you're exercising! It's not as easy as it looks, but the good news is, the more you practise the fitter you'll get. You can grab a hula hoop for less than £5 at your local toystore, they come in neon-fabulous colours and you can either do it with your Pink Ladies or on your own for endless hoopla, keep-fit fun – happy hoopin'!

Masterclass #3
Eat yourself gorgeous!

"...A healthy 'tude to food!..."

My body is not, and never will be, pop-girl shaped. It is, however, Lola-shaped and j'adore it. So when I eat food, I make sure it's the right food.

It's simple really. I dig on me, so it would be completely rude and wrong to fill me up with super-addictive junk food – it's called junk for a reason y'know!

Now I'm not saying I'm perfect-o-girl, I heart food mostest, but when you're Beauty*licious, you have to have a healthy 'tude to food - you eat the right food or, if it's the wrong food, like chocolate, biscuits or takeaways, you eat it as a treat. The payback? A healthier, even-more-gorgeous-if-at-all-possible YOU!

What's your eating style?

Are you a fast food freak or are you nuts for healthy treats?

When you feel hungry, what do you think first?
a. Where's the crisps?
b. I wonder what's in the cupboard?

How often do you have take out?
a. Every week - they're dee-licious!
b. Only as a treat every now and again.

Do you eat 5 portions of fruit or veg a day?
a. Er...Not even, is that bad?
b. I do my best!

When you're out with your Pink Ladies, do you...
a. Order fries right away, I can't resist!
b. Most places offer a healthy option, so I'll opt for that!

How often do you think about your eating style?

a. Not very often, I'll worry about it when I'm older.

b. It's important to eat well at any age, so I try and think about what I put in my body regularly.

Mostly a's

Hey girl, do you know what a piece of fruit actually looks like? While it's fine to eat fast food and chocolate occasionally, you do need to add fresh fruit and veg to your diet. Believe it or not, healthy food can be just as yumsville, so read on and find out what tummy treats will make you truly Beauty*licious...

Mostly b's

Wow, I'm totally impressed at your willpower chica! You tend to avoid most junk food and, instead, tuck into super-healthy fruit and veg. You're doing your body one huge massive Beauty*licious favour with this approach. Try not to worry if you have the odd bar of chocolate – everything in moderation is what being Beauty*licious is all about!

Your 'tude to food

A healthy 'tude to food is completely necessary if you're to become the very best l'il miss Beauty*licious you can possibly be.

Start by saying 'No, Nope, Nopity No' to:

★ **Crazy crash diets that just don't work** – really, they don't and they won't.

★ **Takeaway/fast food/chocolate binges** – binging on bad food is not good for your body or your self-esteem.

★ **Starving yourself** – depriving yourself of food will just make you want it a whole lot more, so when your body eventually gives in, which it always will, chances are you'll overeat the stuff your body craves most, like fatty and sugary foods. Boo.

And instead, say 'Yes, yep, yeppity yep, yes' to:

★ **Listening to your body** – your bod is super-clever and has subtle ways of telling you it disagrees with your food choices.

★ **Eating breakfast** – don't skip breakfast as it will make your stomach growl like a monster-type later in the day.

★ **Healthy food alternatives** – replacing the family pack of biscuits with five servings of fruit or vegetables a day.

Ditch the Diet

Because diets are sucky x 100.

Talk of all things diet-related is going to be ditched right now.

Why?

Because diets are sucky x 100. Especially the A-list style crash diets that promise you a better body in two weeks. They suck mostest. In reality, all diets actually do is make you into a super-grouchy, queen of angst. When you deprive yourself of serious nutrients that your body needs to function, and endlessly calorie-count and scale-jump, it's more than enough to make a girl feel glum, glum, glum about herself. Which, frankly chica, when you're Beauty*licious, is just not an option.

Now, while I hate to admit it, I've been a complete sucker for the crash diet in the past. My worst one was the 'No Carbs' diet, where you basically replace carbohydrates (bread, pasta, rice, potatoes) with high-protein, high-fat foods like meat cheese and eggs. The theory is, your body's fat-burning process turns to high-speed, making you an instant slim-o.

Wrong.

All I got was an achey belly and baaaaad, bad, beyond bad breath. I am not exaggerating when I say people kept a whole lot of distance from me for the entire week that I was doing it. Chica, I hummed!

But that's what happens when you cut something really important out of your diet, your body sends out a message that it's not happy, not one little bit.

You see, carbs aren't the enemy. In fact, 'no-carb' diets aren't good for us girls full stop. Growing bodies need mucho carbs for energy. Diets are bad, so no more mention of them, okay?

You decide!

When you're Beauty*licious, you make the choice about what's right for your sparkly-gorgeous self. You decide whether to devour an entire family sized bar of chocolate in one sitting or whether to, instead, have a couple of chocolate chunks each evening after you've done your homework as an extra-special bite-sized treat. You're in control sweet thing. Yep, your Pink Ladies will always look out for you, but ultimately, you're responsible for number one – you.

I was the official chow-down chick when it came to eating an entire king-sized bar in one sitting. I would go into a chocolate-induced trance, not even tasting it until the final bite. That was because I was living in I-don't-dig-me-ville. Every time I felt sad and glum about not having friends, or the size of my bee-hind, I would throw myself a full-blown pity-party and would make myself feel better by chomping on chocolate. I would instantly feel allsorts of guilty and turn into my very own number one hater, dissing on myself so bad that I'd have to go eat another bar of chocolate.

Yep, your Pink Ladies will always look out for you, but ultimately, you're responsible for number one – you.

Life was not at all sweet.

That was until my world turned substantially pinker and I developed a kick-ass Beauty*licious 'tude. I soon realised that I was fabulousness in a me-shaped package and that I was the one in control. Yep, I could decide to eat a king-sized chocolate bar, but I could also decide not to as well. It was a Think Pink Beauty*licious revelation!

I got sad about everything

Yummy-In-My-Tummy

Making the right eating decisions is quite possibly the nicest thing you can do for your Beauty*licious self, so treat your tummy by following the devised-by-Pink-Ladies: Beauty*licious 'Yummy-in-my-tummy' Plan. You'll find out what foods do what and why, you'll turbo-boost your energy levels and improve your complexion, hair and nails. Anything that makes you feel AND look Beauty*licious has got to be worth a try, hasn't it?

ladies wot lunch

Dear Diary

Writing down everything you eat and drink and your matching moods is a super-cool way to get to know your own eating habits and to check out how healthy you really are. Be honest now...

What you will need:

* ✷ A bag-sized exercise book – that way you'll be able to carry it with you everywhere you go
* ✷ A pen – to write with, silly!
* ✷ Decorating material – not at all necessary, I just love an art project!

Instructions:

1. Optional extra: cover your food diary so it looks good enough to eat! Although please try to remember, at times of hunger, that it is only a diary and not a food item.

Eating it could lead to allsorts of icky digestion problems and you'd have to repeat this whole process again. Not good.

2. Write at the top of each page the days of the week, then under each day start recording everything you eat.

3. Keep a note of your feelings too, this can be really good to identify certain food triggers. For example, if I eat fast food fries, I get a yucky stomach ache almost instantly – I didn't connect the two at first but it wasn't until I kept a food diary that I saw they were related. No more fries = one pain-free star jumping Lola – yay!

4. After the first week, take a look back at what you've been munching. Are you eating enough? Too much? Are you snacking on bad stuff? The diary is a great way to help you see in black and white what's actually going in to your body and will help you pin-point areas you may need to work on.

	MONDAY...............	TUESDAY...............	WEDNESDAY....
Breakfast	Ate: Feeling:	Ate: Feeling:	Ate: Feeling:
Lunch	Ate: Feeling:	Ate: Feeling:	Ate: Feeling:
Dinner	Ate: Feeling:	Ate: Feeling:	Ate: Feeling:

HURSDAY............	FRIDAY............	SATURDAY............	SUNDAY............
te:	Ate:	Ate:	Ate:
eeling:	Feeling:	Feeling:	Feeling:
te:	Ate:	Ate:	Ate:
eeling:	Feeling:	Feeling:	Feeling:
te:	Ate:	Ate:	Ate:
eeling:	Feeling:	Feeling:	Feeling:

Recipe for success

If you're diggin' on how your body feels, then the chances are you're filling it with feel-good treats on a regular basis. But if you're body is flashing a huge 'help me out here' sign, the trick is to make a change...right now.

For real Beauty*licious body-lovin' success it's all about the balance. Not the kind that involves standing on one leg, because that would just result in a Pink Lady floor mess. Nope, this kind will make sure your body gets all the fabness it needs to rock out on a daily basis.

The Yummy-In-My-Tummy ingredients:

Carbohydrates
These fill-you-up foods provide you with the turbo boost energy you need to keep you going all day long.

WHERE YOU CAN GET IT: bread, rice, pasta, lentils and potatoes are all excellent carb providers. For the best energy hit, go for wholegrain carbs – such as brown rice, bread and pasta – because they release energy slowly and will keep you doing star-jumps for longer.

Protein
This is super-essential for the growth and repair of your body, so you need plenty while you're growing into the most Beauty*licious version of you.

WHERE YOU CAN GET IT: meat and fish are great for protein – aim for between two to four portions of oily fish (like salmon and mackerel) a week for the best nutritional hit.

Veggie-girls can choose from pulses, nuts, tofu and eggs.

Fruit and Veg

These are full of the essential vitamins and minerals your body needs. Big grown-up studies show that getting plenty in your diet can protect you from icky illnesses.

WHERE YOU CAN GET IT: it's best to eat fresh fruit and raw vegetables, but fruit juices, smoothies, dried fruit and frozen veg all count too!

Iron

This mineral is mucho important for us girls as we can experience an iron deficiency when our periods start. Iron helps to make red blood cells, which are vital for transporting blood around our bodies.

WHERE YOU CAN GET IT: leafy vegetables like spinach and watercress, plus meat, especially liver and kidneys. Wholegrains, fortified breakfast cereals, nuts and dried fruit are also top sources.

Calcium

This mineral helps build strong bones and teeth so that we're able to practise our killer smile at every opportunity. It also keeps our heart beating, which has got to be a good thing, right?

WHERE YOU CAN GET IT: milk, cheese and yoghurt have plenty. You can also find it in green veg like broccoli and cabbage and in fish with edible bones like sardines and pilchards. This is super-essential for the growth and repair of your body, so you need plenty while you're growing.

The Yummy-In-My-Tummy Munchin' Marvels

You're smart chica, you know junk food is bad for you, so why don't you make like the Pink Ladies and create your very own 'munchin' marvels' – mix and match meals that taste dee-licious and will make your body want to kiss your belly from the inside.

Come eat with us!

Beauty Licious Breakfasts

Butt-kick your body into action each morning with these:

Feeling fruity – trade your frosted flakes for a bowl of muesli with semi-skimmed milk. Tuck into an apple and finish with a glass of unsweetened pure orange juice.

Nuts for nuts – smear two slices of wholemeal toast lightly with peanut butter and put a sliced banana on top (a Lola special!).

Shake-tastic – pour half a pint of semi-skimmed milk, your favourite fruit and one pot of yoghurt in a blender. Whizz it all together for your very own vitamin-packed shake!

Lola's Lunches

'Do' lunch with your Pink Ladies the healthy way:

Bag a bagel - cram a bagel with cream cheese and sliced tomato. Follow with a yoghurt, two pieces of fruit and a carton of unsweetened juice.

Sarnie-time – fill two slices of granary bread with ham and salad. Finish off with two pieces of fruit, a treat-sized chocolate bar – yay! And a glass of water.

Pitta Patter - fill a wholemeal pitta bread with half a tin of tuna and salad. Follow it up with yoghurt, a piece of fruit and water.

Food facts and Dee-lish Dinners

Take away, shmake away! Try these healthy dinners instead:

Chicken Tonight – munch a grilled chicken breast and baked potato with lots of steamed veg.

Some like it hot - if you dig spicy food, gulp down some steaming chilli made with lean mince, peppers and kidney beans, served with rice, grated cheese and salad.

Perfect Pasta – a homemade lasagne with a large side-salad is a treat at dinnertime. For a pudding, why not go old school and have a bowl of banana with fresh custard – now that's what I'm talking about!

'Scuse the breath!

A great way to detox your body is to eat plenty of onions and garlic. They're also great for keeping cold and flu away, too – let's just hope it doesn't have the same effect on cute boys!

Make friends with Muesli

Your body won't thank you for skipping brekkie especially when you stuff your face with crisps at 11am 'cause you're starving. Eating first thing boosts your energy levels – go without and you'll suffer a slump in concentration, too.

Calorie bustin'

If you regularly bust moves on the dance floor, you'll burn around 300 calories an hour – which is as much as a slice of pepperoni pizza. Look how long you'd have to shake it to burn off the following foods:

Cheese and onion crisps (184 calories): 36 minutes 46 seconds
A Big Mac (492 calories): 98 minutes 24 seconds
Fries, regular (207 calories): 41 minutes 24 seconds
Can of coke (139 calories): 27 minutes 48 seconds
Jam doughnut (336 calories): 67 minutes 12 seconds

So, conjure your TV chef of choice (mine is definitely Nigella Lawson, she rocks) and work your very own marvellous 'munchin marvels'. Remember, you don't have to be perfect when it comes to food – just be aware of what you're eating - food is fabulous after all.

Munchin' Marvels

Created by...
(Insert your very own chef name here. For inspir-o, mine is L'il Miss Chocolate Saucepot!)

Breakfast

....
....
....
....
....
....
....
....
....
....
....
....
....
....
....
....
....
....
....
....
....

Lunch

....
....
....
....
....

Dinner

Mood Foods

Eat yourself Beauty*licious with these super-food fixes that will have you glowing inside and out...

Fruit = glow-girl skin
For skin that sparkles, star-shine girl, eat lots of berries – strawberries, blueberries and blackberries. They contain anti-oxidants which protect skin cells from damage and help make you look all glow-girl!

Oily fish = luxe locks
Eating salmon, sardines, tuna or mackerel will keep your hair as shiny as one of those badly dubbed girls on the shampoo adverts. These fish contain lots of protein and omega-3 fatty acids, which moisturise your tresses from within. Happy hair swishing!

Oats and nuts = energy
Swap sugary-sweet cereal for porridge – it's the perfect start to the day. Porridge is fabbity fab because it releases energy slowly and will keep away those mid-morning chocolate cravings.

Bananas = happy belly
Poorly digested food can sit in your belly and make you feel allsorts of icky but the potassium in a banana will mop up excessive fluids reducing any uncomfy feelings. No more impromptu exits from fab soirees due to ickster bellies – yay!

Are you missing out?

Pink Lady, Sadie, put her stressy, messy head down to the fact that exams were looming. Except, it didn't go away after the exams. In fact, Sadie felt so unbelievably un-fabulous that her parentals sent her straight to the doctor...

"...I WAS GETTING A HURTY HEAD EVERY DAY AND WAS SO TIRED I JUST COULDN'T GET UP. I FOUND IT DIFFICULT TO CONCENTRATE IN LESSONS THAT WEREN'T EVEN MATHS AND EVERYONE WAS COMMENTING ON HOW WELL I WAS WORKING THE WHOLE KELLY-O PALE GIRL LOOK.

"APPARENTLY, PALE IS NOT JUST THE SIGN OF A TOTALLY ACCEPTABLE FASHION CHOICE. ACCORDING TO THE DOCTOR DUDE, IT'S ALSO A SIGN, ALONG WITH TIREDNESS AND LACK OF CONCENTRATION THAT I COULD BE SHORT OF IRON. I MEAN, WHO KNEW?

"US CHICAS ARE MORE AT RISK OF BEING LOW IN IRON BECAUSE YOU'RE STILL GROWING AND DEVELOPING.

"DOCTOR DUDE TO THE RESCUE THOUGH – HE SAYS IT'S REALLY RATHER EASY TO GET ENOUGH IRON. JUST AVOID DRINKING TEA OR COFFEE AT MEALTIMES BECAUSE THESE REDUCE THE AMOUNT OF IRON WE ABSORB FROM FOOD AND, INSTEAD, EAT FRESH FRUIT, TOMATOES OR DRINK FRUIT JUICE (ALL OF WHICH CONTAIN VITAMIN C) WITH MEALS AS THEY HELP THE BODY ABSORB THE IRON IN FOOD – WE LOVE YOU DOCTOR DUDE!"

Sadie didn't think that what she was or wasn't eating could have such an icky impact on her health. But what w put in our bodies can affect us both inside and out. If you eat junk, your energy levels will be super-low and make you feel like a lame-o version of yourself. But if you drink a lot of water each day, your skin will be smooth and clear.

When you take maximum care of your body and fill it with all the right food, it'll repay you by making you jump-in-the-air fabulous – pretty good deal really, isn't it?

> According to the doctor dude, paleness is also a sign, along with tiredness and lack of concentration, that I could be short of iron.

Snack Attack!

I'm all about eating 'little and often' which makes snacking a completely do-able activity – yay! Snacks keep your body ticking over. But what you choose to snack on is crucial to the success of your tummy feeling yummy. When you get a snack attack, don't dip in the biscuit jar – get a load of these treats instead:

✫ Handful of dried fruit or nuts – a feel-good fill up!

✫ Bowl of wholegrain cereal with semi-skimmed milk – not just for breakfast you know!

✫ Plain popcorn – cinema trip optional.

✫ Scoop of frozen yoghurt – like ice cream but without the fat – the stuff that dreams are made of!

✫ Raw vegetables – have a bowl ready-chopped in the fridge for when the munchies strike. Try dipping those raw vegetables in some home-made holy-moly guacamole! It's made out of Avocados which are great for you as they're low in saturated fat and taste totally yumsville too.

What you'll need to make your own holy-moly guacamole...
✫ Two large ripe avocados
✫ Three cloves of crushed garlic
✫ 1/2 finely chopped onion
✫ Juice of a lemon

Cut each avocado in half, remove the pit. (the big maa-seeve stone in the middle) Scoop the flesh out and mash in a bowl with a fork. Add the garlic, onion and juice, mix and season with pepper. Mmmmm.

The problem
So you're feeling hungry?
Try eating...
Oats, beans, peas
Why?
Foods with fibre are more bulky and help us feel fuller for longer

The problem
Do you need energy?
Try eating...
Bananas, jacket potatoes, pasta
Why?
Starchy foods are a great source of energy and the main source of a range of nutrients

The problem
Want strong teeth and bones?
Try eating...
Milk, cheese, watercress
Why?
For strong teeth and bones, our bodies need calcium and Vitamin D

The problem
Want to top up your iron levels?
Try eating...
Red meats, beans and pulses and green veg
Why?
Symptoms of iron deficiency include tiredness and trouble concentrating – now Sadie is eating lots of green leafy veg, her symptoms are practically non-existant!

The Pink Ladies Yummy-In-My-Tummy tips

★ If you rely on your parentals for the food you eat and you want to make a change, have a chat to them about it. Angel's mumma makes killer Caribbean food. But there's only so much fried chicken, rice and peas a girl can handle without feeling like she might burst at her too-cute jean seams. So Angel, careful not to hurt her mumma's feelings, explained to her that as yummy as her food was, she'd like to only have the fried dinner as a special treat once a week and shared some of her Beauty*licious nutrition facts with her – the Angel household is a whole lot healthier and happier because of it.

★ Eating two fist-sized portions of either meat, chicken, fish, eggs or beans a day will help to build and repair skin cells as well as making your nails strong enough for a totally jaw-dropping two coat application of Brighton Rock pink nail varnish. Rock out, chica!

★ Cut down on fatty and sugary food but don't cut them out all together – woohoo. A little bit of everything is good for you and if you deny yourself something totally, you'll just crave it even more. It just wouldn't be possible for me never to have chocolate ever again and, luckily, I don't have to. See, being Beauty*licious is really rather fabulous!

★ While it may seem boring snoring, drinking loads of water - at least eight glasses a day cleanses your insides and is by far the best way to fast-track yourself to a spot-free complexion.

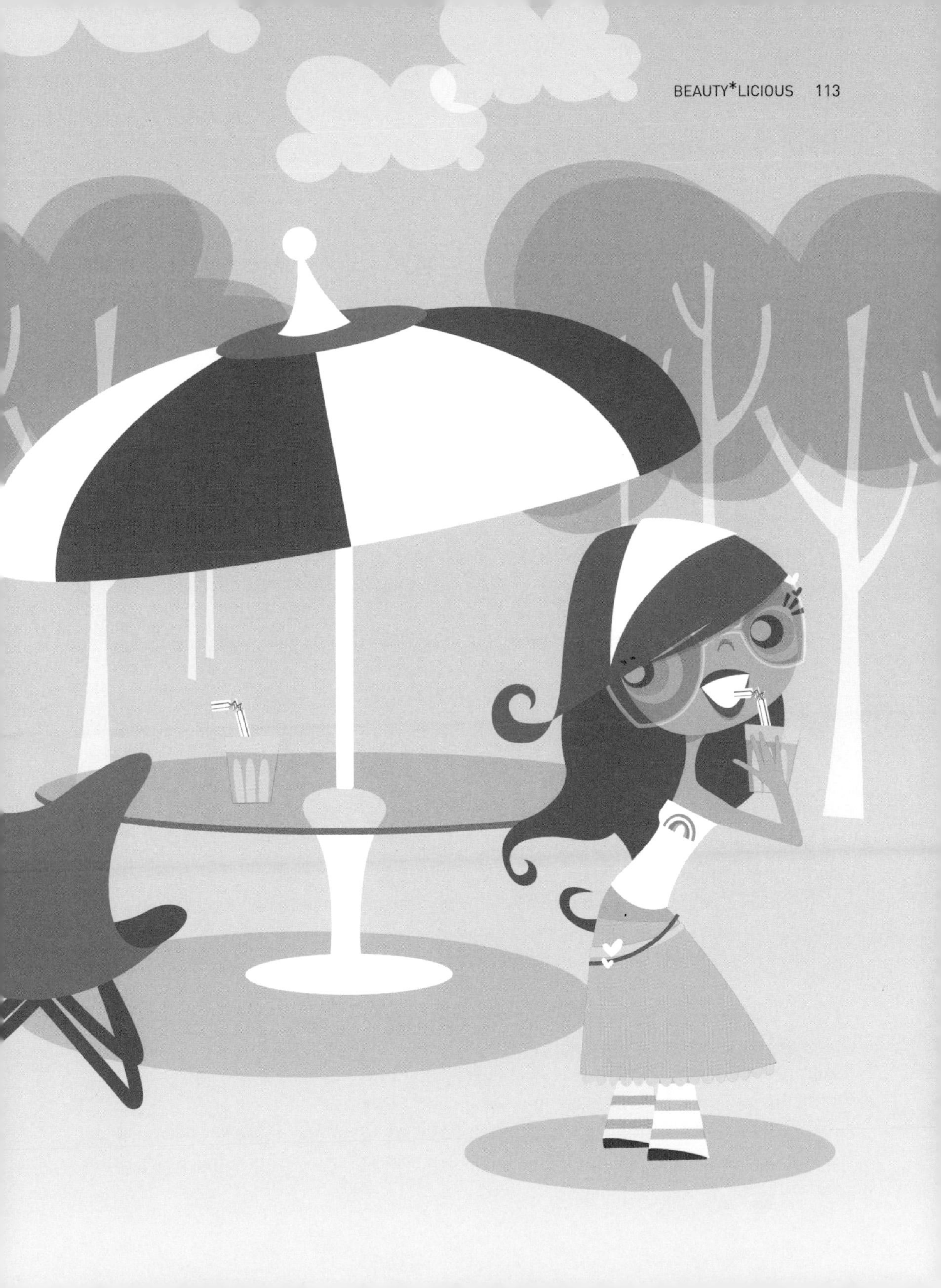

The Beauty'licious Parlour

You ask the questions, we'll provide the buffet.

Exercise makes me feel really hungry and sometimes I end up eating more than I did previously, what can I do?

THE PINK LADIES: You're hungry because exercise switches your energy level to 'go girl' pace and your body is burning the food you ate earlier at a much faster rate. Leave two hours after a meal before exercise, that way your body has some stored energy to work with. If you're hungry after a workout, snack on healthy treats like a banana or a handful of nuts.

During after-school activities, my tummy lets out really embarrassing growls – how can I stop it?

THE PINK LADIES: Sounds like you're so super-busy that you sometimes forget to eat until your stomach starts growling like crazy. Going long stretches without food can lead to big-time energy slumps and can mean you're missing the vitamins, minerals and other good stuff your body needs. Make sure you make time to eat before your tummy sends out a Beauty*licious SOS.

So, I've got a friend coming over for tea but she says she only eats 'organic' food. What is 'organic' exactly?

THE PINK LADIES: Organic is all about the way food is grown. Organic farmer-types fear that nasty chemicals used in normal farming, like fertiliser and pesticides, can be harmful to humans and the environment over a long period of time. So they don't use any chemicals at all when growing their food. They rely on healthy soil to produce food that can resist pests and diseases. Most supermarkets now offer an organic selection of food covering everything from fruit and veg to chocolate and cereal – why don't you ask your friend to go shopping with you before you go home for tea?

I don't like water, is there anything else I can drink?

THE PINK LADIES: Water may seem boring snoring, but it's the ultimate Beauty*licious ingredient and here's why: diet drinks may say they have no sugar but they contain artificial sweeteners which can be just as bad for you as real sugar. Water is totally calorie-free and glugging eight glasses a day boosts concentration, relieves tiredness and keeps your internal organs working, no Beauty*licious girl is seen without it!

you should snack
on healthy treats

Masterclass #4
Darn, you're pretty

"...Beautification - because you're worth it!..."

I make no apologies.

I am a make-up wearing, product-loving Beautista who hearts nothing more than to beautify my sweet self on a daily basis.

Facials, trimming my fringe, applying copious amounts of 'vibrant violet' glitter dust to my eyelids and painting my tippy toes a shocking shade of pink are just a few of my most favourite ways to spend a day. Because chica, beautification is not a self-indulgent afterthought - it's an act of extreme Beauty*liciousness!

Are you lovin' your looks?

Do you dig on your looks or run from your reflection?

How often do you look in the mirror during the day?
a. Hmm, I don't really think about it – maybe once or twice?
b. Three or four times. You know, just to re-apply my gloss and check on my hair.

You're getting ready for school, it's:
a. Super easy! I just pull my hair into a ponytail and go.
b. A bit of a production! It's a bit stressy, but I have so much fun getting creative with my looks to show off my personality.

A professional manicure is:
a. The name of a major league lame-o boy band?
b. A weekly nail treat that makes me drool over the complete gorgeousness of my own hands!

What's the one beauty item you simply cannot live without?
a. Lip balm – dry lips are sucky x100.
b. Just one? That's impossible!

You're in town, when you and your Pink Ladies head for the nearest beauty counter. You feel:
a. Completely overwhelmed – when can I get out of here?
b. Just look at the rows of eyeshadows and lipglosses – I. MUST. HAVE. EVERYTHING!

Mostly a's
While 'au naturel' is such a good look, it's one of many that you can experiment with when you're Beauty*licious, chica! Not only is a prettification routine fun, most importantly, it can provide you with a huge Beauty*licious bravado boost on a daily basis. Now, what's not to love about that?

Mostly b's
Girl, you and your looks have got a healthy relationship going on. You definitely know how to work your Beauty*licious self around a beauty counter and, while your appearance matters, you know it's not everything – a sure sign that you're rockin' your way to Beauty*liciousness!

we love you professional manicure
duh, they're not a real band ya know!

The Temple of YOU

You ever heard that saying 'your body is a temple'?

Well, when you're Beauty*licious, you worship at the 'temple of You' everyday.

What we do to our body, or put into it, is a reflection of how much we dig ourselves. So, it makes a whole lot of sense that if you want to look and feel fierce and fabulous, you have to treat your body with respect and keep it in perfecto working order. Right?

Which is why the Pink Ladies and I worship our fabulousness by staring in the mirror, primping and experimenting daily with various Beauty*licious routines. Not only is it a major source of fun, it's a chance to play goddess-girl with our appearance, max up our self image and gives us that super-important moment of the day to say: "Hey Gorgeous Girl – you're looking seriously Beauty*licious!"

You see, a true Beauty*licious Beautista will work her beauty routine out of pure prettifying pleasure not out of self-loathing. She doesn't put make-up on to cover up, she puts it on to enhance her too-cute features because pampering is all about the fun. If you enjoy looking after yourself, other people will pick up on your positive 'tude and you will become a walking, talking, primping, preening poster girl for all things Beauty*licious – damn, you're pretty!

What's your ultimate beauty treat to yourself?

....

....

....

....

....

....

....

....

....

....

....

....

Which hair products do you dig?

....

....

....

....

....

....

....

....

....

....

....

....

....

....

List your five must-have beautification products...

....

....

....

....

....

....

....

....

....

....

....

....

....

....

....

....

....

Glam Girl Squad

Meet the Glam Girl squad. Your very own go-girl team dedicated to making you feel as feisty, fun, fearless and fabulous as you can possibly be. Okay, so it's us, the Pink Ladies, but you know how much we love to play dress up... and you're nevah-evah too old to play dress up!

The Glam Girl Squad are the perfect accessory for any wannabe beautista, not only do we come in super-cute Grease-inspired costumes - ankle socks, big skirts and girly detailing with matching candy-coloured vanity cases – natch, we are product junkies. In fact, Angel, who is the official tiara-wearing product princess, knows exactly what they all are and what they do. Together, we're your Beautification 101, sweet thing!

The Glam Girl Squad code of practice:

✭ Always express your feisty, fun, fearless and fabulousness – you know you're all these things no matter what look you're working, right?

✭ Never blend - instead of covering up what's different about you: experiment, ignore trends and figure out how to accentuate your fabness so you'll be sure to stand out in a crowd.

✭ Rock a look that feels completely right for you. If you take the chance to be seen, it doesn't matter if no one else digs it. You're a star-shaped, glitter-girl baby and you call the shots on how you look in your world.

We are the Glam
Girl Squad

The Glam Girl Squad salon

Angel's boudoir is the Academy's official super-salon and in keeping with our 50's inspired theme, pays major homage to all things Americana. Think chrome American diners, strawberry milkshakes and waitress-girl style and you'll have a pretty good idea of the Glam Girl Squad's Beautification HQ.

Now, we are the first to admit that, quite frankly, rules are made to be broken, but when it comes to becoming the most Beauty*licious version of you, the Glam Girl Squad have devised drama-free hair and beauty principle prettifiers that will help you to discover and celebrate your own YOUnique Beauty*licious beauty style.

Skin Deep

Beauty*licious beautification starts with your skin. And glow-girl skin comes from within. Your skin is a super-sized billboard advertisement for what's going on in your body. If your diet is junky or you're not drinking enough water, your skin will tell the world in the forms of blemishes, blotches, open pores and general ickyness. Not good.

To avoid becoming a complexion disaster, don't give your skin a single excuse to break out.

✶ **Don't smoke -** not only does it give you stinky breath, it gives you wrinkles and dull skin – yuck.

✶ **Opt for Kelly-O pale –** as cute as a sun tan may look, the effects of the sun's rays on your skin are totally harmful – I apply sunscreen every day, even when it's not sunny, securing my future as a baby-faced 50-year-old! If you're all about the beach babe look use a bronzer or self-tanner, both give instant colour without the risk of skin cancer or wrinkles.

✶ **Don't touch your face –** your fingertips are home to more pimple-producing oils than you could ever imagine. So no matter how tempting it might be to pop the mini-volcano that's threatening to erupt on your chin – **DON'T.**

✶ **Routine -** your skin-care routine should become as much a part of your daily process as brushing your teeth. And, the best thing? You don't need ridiculously over-priced products to scrub up well – they may come in super-swanky packaging but all that sets them apart from the beauty store's own-brand version is their mucho-inflated price tag.

For gorgeous-girl skin, make this your twice-daily Beauty*licious three step process:
1. **Cleanse –** use a super-gentle cleanser to wash your face and remove all the dirt and impurities, rinse with warm water.
2. **Tone -** a toner is used to refresh the skin and mops up any dirt that the cleanser may have left behind, apply with cotton wool.
3. **Moisturise –** to keep our skin in tip-top-tutti-frutti condition we need to plump up the skin cells with moisture – pat it on your skin instead of smoothing it on. This increases circulation and boosts your complexion big time.

quad Prettifier

...ess and treat your skin to a weekly facial. It'll thank you by giving you a Glam Girl glow – sounds like a pretty good deal to us!

You will need:
* Use of the bathroom
* Exfoliating scrub – a cream with little scrubbers that gets rid of dead skin
* A towel
* Mud mask

Instructions:
* Tie your hair back and remove any make-up with a face wipe.
* Wet your face and massage an exfoliating scrub over your skin. Rinse off with warm water.
* Put hot (not boiling) water into a bowl, hold face above it and cover head with a towel – this will loosen up any pore-clogging dirt.
* After four minutes, pat skin dry with towel and apply a deep cleansing mask, lie down and relax!
* Wait five minutes then wipe mask away with cotton wool pads dipped in warm water.
* Finish with a light layer of moisturiser to protect and hydrate your skin.

Spot Check

Zits are rude. Fact.

They always seem to appear before that really important date with dream dude and, for that reason alone, I detest them. Yet, no matter how hard I try to devise a pink magic sparkle wand to wave those pesky zits goodbye forever, they still keep coming back for more – grrr.

Time for the science bit: spots appear when the tiny holes that super-fine hair grows from get blocked by dirt that sticks to the natural oils produced by our skin. Blocked follicles look like tiny dots – blackheads. But when these get infected they turn into white heads – real life, boo-worthy spots.

Now it may be hard to believe, but Pink Lady, and Glam Girl Squad member, Bella, used to be a maxim-o shy girl and would avoid going out and seeing people because of her spots...

"...I HAD ACNE AND I FELT SUPER-EMBARRASSED BECAUSE EVERYONE ELSE SEEMED TO HAVE MODEL-ESQUE SKIN. I FELT REALLY UNCOMFY WITH MYSELF AND SOME PEOPLE TEASED ME. I TRIED NOT TO TAKE ANY NOTICE, BUT IT HURT. I FELT LIKE PEOPLE WERE ALWAYS LOOKING AT ME AND LAUGHING. IT WAS REALLY PRETTY SUCKSVILLE ACTUALLY.

"I TRIED EVERYTHING TO BLITZ THEM - ANTI-BACTERIAL SPOT CREAMS, WASHES AND FACIAL MASKS. ALTHOUGH THEY WORKED ON MY FRIEND'S OCCASIONAL PIMPLES, MY SPOTS WOULD DISAPPEAR FOR A DAY, BUT WOULD ALWAYS COME BACK EVEN WORSE – HOW RUDE IS THAT?

"I FELT NO ONE ELSE HAD SPOTS AS BAD AS ME. I DIDN'T WANT TO DO ANYTHING. I DIDN'T EVEN WANT TO GO TO SCHOOL. LUCKILY, YOGA DAD DIDN'T LET ME MOPE AROUND FOR LONG. HE WENT ON THE INTERNET AND FOUND REAL-LIFE PRACTICAL THINGS I COULD DO, LIKE INCREASING MY DAILY WATER INTAKE FROM THREE TO FIVE GLASSES, NOT RUBBING MY FACE WHEN I WASHED IT AS THAT IRRITATED THE SKIN, AND TO TAKE DIETARY SUPPLEMENTS LIKE ZINC. MY SKIN IS BY NO MEANS PERFECT-O BUT, OVER THE YEARS, IT HAS REALLY IMPROVED... ALONG WITH MY NEW BEAUTY*LICIOUS ATTITUDE TOWARDS MYSELF – I NOW DIG ON ME LOTS AND LOTS, WITH OR WITHOUT SPOTS!"

I felt no one had spots as bad as me

Bella's spot check

Drink lots of water... the more you drink the better your skin will become.

⭐ **Don't avoid your Pink Ladies –** when my skin was really bad, I didn't have too many friends. I didn't think people would want to know me, I was giraffe-girl tall with a whole lot of spots, why would they? Little did I know that it was actually me pushing people away with my negative vibes about myself. If I'd known my Pink Ladies back then, they'd have definitely been on hand to give me a Beauty*licious bravado boost – yours will be too!

⭐ **Ignore any nasty-rude comments –** if someone gets all shouty in your direction, ignore them. You know you're fabulous; you don't need validation, sweet thing!

⭐ **Drink lots of water –** at the risk of sounding like a CD stuck on repeat, the more you drink the better your skin will become. Fact.

Glam-Girl Squad: Skin Secrets

Shhhh, don't tell anyone but...

⭐ Double up on your cleanser at night. The first lather removes make up, the second goes deeper making sure your skin is squeaky-clean and blemish free.

⭐ Use a gentle exfoliator twice a week to prevent dirt-clogged pores.

⭐ Get your heart pumping with some shape throwing on the dance floor – it'll give you that healthy flush and will make your skin look ah-mazing. Falling in crush with a dream dude works too. Whatever's easiest, sweet thing!

To find out your skin type, blot a tissue over your un-made up, unwashed face.
Greasy all over = oily skin.
No grease = dry skin.
Greasy in the centre only = combination skin.

Not sure how much product to use? It really is up to you but here's the GGS guide to dollop sizes:
Cleanser – cherry size
Scrub – 50p size
Moisturiser – fruit pastille size
Face mask – conker size
Spot gel – peanut size

Skincare doesn't need to be pricey. Cheaper products often contain exactly the same ingredients. There's really no reason why you should spend over a fiver on anything.

Hip, hip hair-ay!

I have not got enough day-glo pink manicured fingers to count how many times I've been in a 'ohmystars, I'm having a bad-hair-day' crisis. It's by far the saddest of states a girl can find herself in. Which is why, when you're Beauty*licious, you don't have to because you simply say bah-bye to bad hair days and make the most of your 'do.

Coolio eh?

If you don't like your hair, change it. It really is as simple as that. My hair used to be every shade of bland, untouched and completely lacking in any kind of glamourised Beauty*liciousness, that was until wannabe hairstylist Bella attacked me with a shocking shade of pink hair dye. I haven't looked back since. It's a fact that my life is significantly more fabulous when my hair matches my mood! It's only temporary too, so if I were to ever enter into a red 'Electra' phase, or a goth-girl-black phase – not that I ever would, but if I were to, it would all be completely do-able at the turn of a water tap!

What's you dream hairstyle?

....
....
....
....
....
....
....
....
....

What colour would you love your hair to be?

....
....
....
....
....
....
....
....

Stick a photo or draw a pic of your dream 'do here

Work up a lather

Make sure your hair wash is as Glam-Girl-tastic as it is at the salon by:

* ☆ Never using bathwater to rinse your hair – that's just plain icksville.

* ☆ Using the pads of your fingers to massage the shampoo right down to the root – not only does it feel really good, it stimulates hair growth to give you Rapunzel-esque locks.

* ☆ Keeping you hair as squeaky-clean as your doll-like face. Shampooing gets rid of all the dirt your hair collects throughout the day, so don't be lazy, make sure washing your hair is on your daily 'to-do' list.

* ☆ Only applying conditioner from the middle of your hair down to the ends. Applying it at the root will equal limp-like locks. Not good.

* ☆ Not being brand loyal – your hair is really rather clever and can get used to your usual hair-cleaning product. Get into the habit of alternating from one week to the next.

Detangling Dos

Do you get killer knots after washing and tug at them relentlessly to work them free? Don't. It's bad. Stop tugging and get rid of knots the right way.

* ☆ Smooth shampoo down your strands when washing instead of piling your hair on top of your head.

* ☆ Dry your hair by squeezing it – not rubbing it – with a soft towel.

* ☆ Use a wide tooth comb to ease out knots. Start from the ends and work towards the roots (brushing from the roots down can cause more tangles and breakage.)

Prettifier: The perfect blow-dry

...sleek, shiny tresses every time...

What you will need:
- ✮ Use of the bathroom
- ✮ Anti-frizz shampoo and conditioner
- ✮ Towel
- ✮ Hair mousse
- ✮ A round bristle brush
- ✮ Hairdryer
- ✮ Glossing spray

Instructions
- ✮ Wash hair with shampoo and conditioner - remember to rinse thoroughly.

- ✮ Squeeze mousse into your hand and distribute through the mid-length and ends of your hair.

- ✮ To make styling easier, divide your hair into sections and fix into place with clips.

- ✮ Place a round bristle brush underneath your hair then blow-dry down the length.

- ✮ To give a softer finish, curl the brush under as you reach the ends of your hair and repeat until hair is dry and finish with a quick spritz of glossing spray.

Time to style
Which products are right for super-stylin' your hair?

Dry hair – Use a smoothing balm or cream. This tames and calms hair that wants to rebel!

Frizzy hair – Applied to wet hair, a serum will lock in moisture, leaving curls totally frizz-free.

Lank Hair – Use a light volume-boosting spray to add ommph without weighing your hair down.

lovin' my shiny locks

Afro-tastic

When you next feel like throwing a hissyfit of epic proportions because that hair kink is just not bustable, spare a thought for Angel and her Afro...

"...AFRO HAIR IS HELLA HIGH MAINTENANCE AND, UNTIL RECENTLY, MUMMA WOULD YANK AND PULL MY HAIR INTO SCALP-TIGHT, BEE-HIND TOUCHING BRAIDS. NOW, I LOVED MY BRAIDS, AND WAS MORE THAN CAPABLE OF WORKING THEM LIKE THEY WERE LONG, BLONDE PRINCESS CURLS. BUT HAVING HAD THEM ALL MY LIFE, I WAS SCARED OF WHAT PEOPLE MIGHT SAY IF THEY WERE TO ACTUALLY SEE ME IN ALL MY AFRO-GLORY. I WOULDN'T EVEN SHOW THE PINK LADIES — THE BRAIDS HAD BECOME SO MUCH A PART OF ME THAT I THOUGHT I MIGHT NOT FIT IN WITHOUT THEM — SILLY, EH?

"NOW I'M BEAUTY*LICIOUS, HOWEVER, HEAD HURT IS NO LONGER A DO-ABLE OPTION AND I KEEP IT REAL. MY AFRO IS OFFICIALLY BIGGER THAN A HOUSE AND, NOW I'M NO LONGER SEEKING APPROVAL, I GET ALLSORTS OF FABULOUS ATTENTION WHICH, BEING THE DIVA-IN-TRAINING THAT I AM, I SIMPLY ADORE!

"AN AFRO IS HARD TO MAINTAIN AND MEANS I HAVE TO GET UP A WHOLE HOUR BEFORE MY ENTIRE HOUSEHOLD TO ENSURE AMPLE BATHROOM TIME. I HAVE TO MAKE SURE I'M AS AFRO-TASTIC AS I CAN POSSIBLY BE — A SMALL PRICE TO PAY TO MAX MY BEAUTY*LICIOUSNESS EACH DAY!"

Angel's 'fro care

★ Afro hair needs to be treated with respect. When it comes to your weekly shampoo ritual, choose a gentle nourishing shampoo that will give it the much-needed moisture it desires.

★ Use a deep-conditioning treatment once or twice a week, depending on the length and condition of your hair. A revitalising treatment will work wonders for dry hair and scalp.

★ Natural bristle brushes are best for relaxed hair and wide-toothed combs for curly styles. Try to keep hot-brush and curling-tong usage to a minimum and always use a heat-protectant product first.

Angel always hated what her mum did to her hair!

Tress SOS

Bad hair CAN happen to good people and is completely capable of making your day less than pink, sparkly fantastical. The good news? Well – duh – you're Beauty*licious, sweet thing, which means you have access to the Glam-Girl Squad's pink vanity case of workable hair solutions...

HELP! I've got frizzy hair

GGS SOLUTION: Step away from the brush immediately! Instead, invest in some smoothing serum and work it through your hair a section at a time. If you're wearing the curls, twist small pieces of hair around your finger really tight then give them each a tiny tug so they hang all boho-curl like – pretty and frizz free!

HELP! I'm trying to grow my hair but the ends look all tatty

GGS SOLUTION: Even if you're growing your hair, you should still get the ends trimmed every 6-8 weeks to keep them tidy and healthy – it'll make your locks look thicker and healthier. You don't have to pay a fortune. Most hairdressers will do a dry cut. This means you don't get your hair washed and styled. They simply cut it, leaving you to do the fun bit!

HELP! I've got greasy hair and not enough time to wash it every day

GGS SOLUTION: Ohmystars – this product will change your life – powder shampoo. Basically it's a form of talc that absorbs all the grease and makes your hair a whole lot less ick. Sprinkle it at the roots and work it through with your fingers – alternatively, you could just get up earlier, lazy Mazie!

Glam-Girl Squad: Hair Secrets

Shhh, don't tell anyone but...

⭐ If, like me, you're a colour-me-up girl, don't use hair products like mousse, gel or hairspray too often as they all contain colour-stripping alcohol. Boo.

⭐ Get your hair salon-shiny in seconds. Hint: It's all about sealing the cuticle. The main work is done in the shower – apply shampoo to soaking wet hair. Otherwise it won't flow through or rinse out evenly and that will leave your hair dull, dull, dull. Ditto goes for conditioner. Blast your hair with water for an extra 30 seconds after you're sure it's clean. Rinse with the coldest water you can handle to smooth your hair cuticle, making it – duh – shiny!

⭐ So you're tired of your fringe and have decided to grow it out. But it's at the stage when you just can't do anything with it. Don't give in and reach for the scissors! With the help of a few cute accessories, you'll make it through. Start with a messy side parting and sweep you fringe to the side, secure with a clip or hold 'em back with a headband – v.cute.

⭐ Give your hair an 'I'm on holiday' look by adding surfer-girl waves. Wash your hair, towel dry it and then smooth some no-frizz serum through it. Wrap a small strand of hair around two fingers up to your roots, then secure with a Kirby grip – do this all over your head. When it's dry, take all the grips out and rake through with your fingers – voila! It's time to surf some waves!

⭐ Before heading to the hairdresser for a new 'do, upload your picture to one of these websites Clairol.com or thehairstyler.com. You can try out tons of different styles without leaving the house. It's mucho fun - Bella looks too cool with a black and red mo-hawk - and it beats getting a bad cut!

Beautista on a Budget

Beauty*licious beauty queens know that the best beautifying products can be found in the kitchen. The Glam Girl Squad always have a fridge-full of homemade pamper potions to turn each other into fresh-faced, Beauty*licious sparkle girls. So save your pennies for that too-cute pair of sweet-looking pink ballet pumps and whip up your very own prettification potions.

Optional extra: Floor your Pink Ladies by making extra helpings of each fruity treat and make extra pamper products for the *sparty* – You'll find out about that later!

Love your locks
Mix two tablespoons of olive oil and one tablespoon of honey in a plastic container, and then place it in a bowl of hot water to warm up the contents. Massage the mix into your scalp and work through to the ends. Put on a shower cap and, for an extra boost, turn

your hairdryer on and give it a quick blast. After 15 minutes, shower off and wash your hair as normal, finishing off with a light conditioner and a dousing of cold water for extra shine.

Lemonade face moisturiser
For tangy cheeks, combine a beaten egg yolk with two teaspoons of fresh lemon juice and whisk. Gradually add half a cup of olive oil until the mixture thickens. If it gets too thick, add more lemon juice. Massage it into your face after cleansing. Store the mixture in the fridge for four to five days.

Eye shine
Treat your peepers by mixing two teaspoons of chopped cucumber with one tablespoon of powdered milk to make a thick gooey paste. Close your eyes and apply to upper and lower lids. Relax for ten minutes. Remove with cotton wool dipped in warm water.

wearing my fab shower cap!

Oh, make me over!

The coolest thing about being a girl is make-up. Fact.

It's a perfect-o way to shout to the world 'This is me, and I'm fierce!'

Bella is ultra-adventurous with her make-up and says it's much better to experiment with make-up than with smoking or alcohol – she's so wise.

Angel is all about over-the-top 70's disco glamour which gets her into allsorts of trouble at her super-posh boarding school.

Sadie digs the wholesome natural look that has hipster boys lining up to kiss her.

While I, however, well I just love creating the girl I want to be each morning depending on my mood!

Now, make-up is by no means the most important thing about being Beauty*licious. Far from it. But it is a too-cute way of expressing your inner girl and giving you an added Beauty*licious boost of fabulousness and, what's more, playing with your appearance is so much fun. Sure, an awkward tiara-ed slow dance with your dream dude rules, but don't sparkly lashes, fresh skin and plenty of pink make you feel like the real star?

What make-up products do you heart mostest?

....

....

....

....

....

....

....

....

....

....

....

....

boys line up
for Sadie

What's in your bag?

The Glam-Girl Squad have industrial-sized bulging make-up bags packed full-to-the-brim with colour-me-pretty make-up treats – you'd expect nothing less really, would you? The thing is, it's not at all necessary. To paint yourself pretty, for any occasion, a Beauty*licious beautista will need:

★ **Small mirror –** pink, natch.

★ **Tinted moisturiser –** to give you colour without feeling like you're wearing make-up.

★ **Brown/black mascara –** a lashifier will open your eyes and cause a breeze when you flutter. Cute.

★ **Two eye shadows –** don't be afraid to experiment as eye shadow can really make a statement. I'm all about purple with sparkles right now, but it's subject to change at any moment-o!

★ **Lip gloss or stain –** able to turn you into a pout-able princess in nano-seconds.

Anything else is pure decadence and, seeing as I heart all things decadent, I also have:

★ **Eyelash curlers –** they turn my eyelashes into extras from a 1950s film set.

★ **My eyeliner –** because, when I wear it, people are always left wondering what I did to look so pretty.

★ **An emery board -** for broken nail emergencies.

★ **An all over shimmer powder –** because you know how I love to sparkle!

So, what's in your bag?

....

....

....

....

....

How long have you had that?

Sadly make-up doesn't last forever.

Tell that to Pink Lady and Glam Girl Squad member, Bella, and she will weep uncontrollably. You see, Bella is a self-confessed hoarder and, having to part with anything, especially make-up, can cause upset x100. Thing is though, if you keep make-up too long it becomes home to grime and germs, the very stuff that gives you blemishes – ick. So, in case you too suffer from ditching-make-up-phobia, here's the Glam-Girl Squad's make-up life expectancy chart...

Mascara: 3 months – any longer and it'll be too dry and clumpy to ever look nice again.
Foundation/tinted moisturiser: 1 year after you open the bottle or tube
Powder: 1 year
Eye shadow: 6 months to a year
Eyeliner: sharpen regularly to keep clean
Blush: 6 months to a year
Lipstick and gloss: Between 1 and 2 years

Glam Girl Squad masterclass: applying make up

Chica, there really are no rules when applying make-up that's why it's by far the greatest way to spend a day! Still, there are some tried and tested Glam-Girl Squad methods that we're happy to share with you doll-face, coz we're good like that!

What you will need:
- ☆ Your make-up bag and its contents
- ☆ An emery board
- ☆ A mirror
- ☆ An active imagination

Eyes

Eye shadow is all about blending, so instead of using the sponge applicator, use your finger to apply as much or as little as you want to the eyelid.

When applying mascara, hold the wand under your lashes, close to the root, and move it from side to side, slowly twirling it as you go all the way to the tips.

For added drama, use eyeliner. Gently pull your eyelid out to the side so the skin is tight. Then, looking down, draw from the inner to the outer corner of your top lid, staying as close to the lash line as possible.

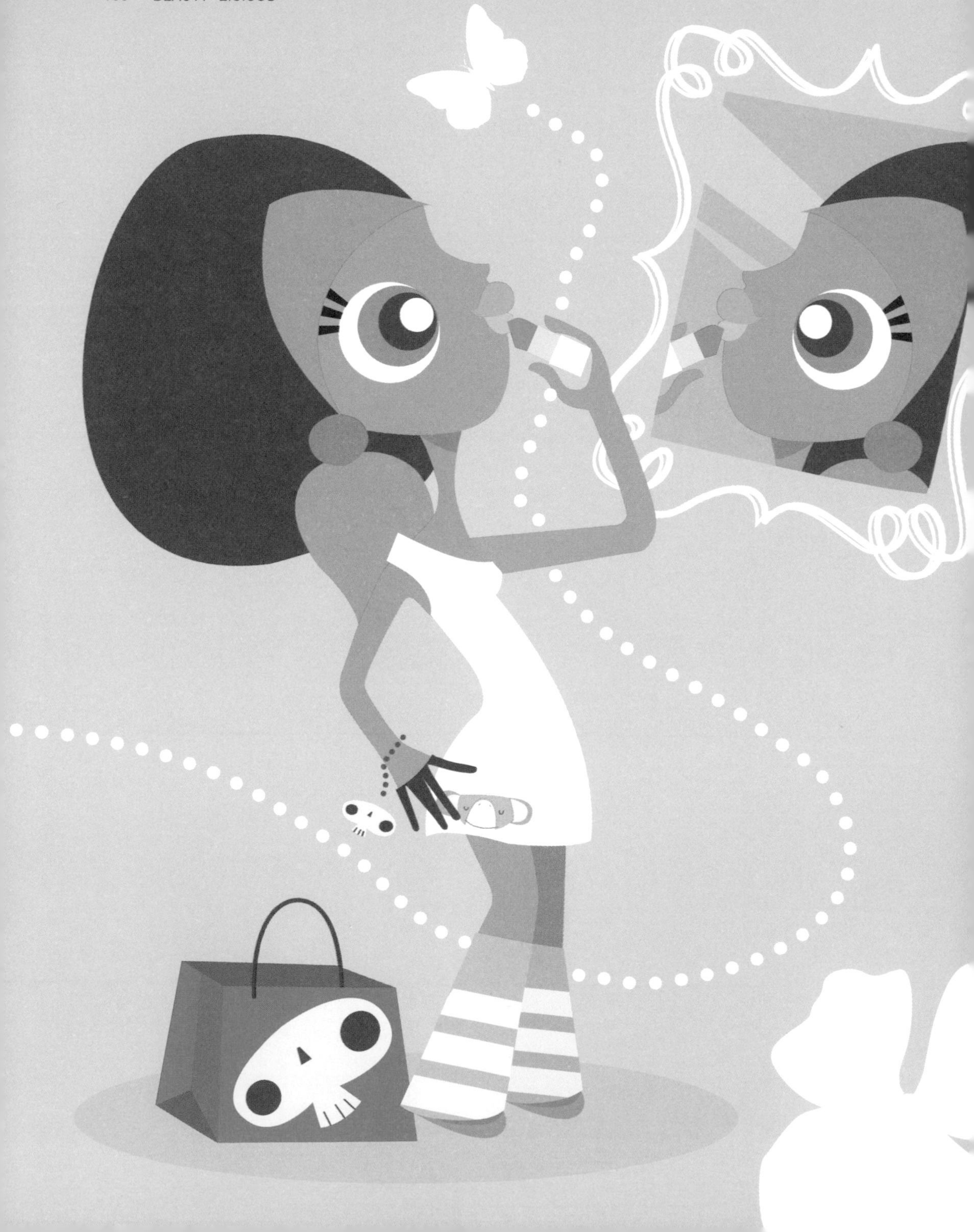

Lips

Lip colour goes on more evenly when applied to a super-smooth surface, so, to get rid of nasty dry bits, slick your lips with petroleum jelly, then rub gently with an old toothbrush. Next, wipe and blot.

Swipe on your favourite gloss and prepare to be amazed at how long your mouth stays this pretty.

Nails

Use an emery board to file nails into a square-round kinda shape. Be sure to only move the board in one direction – filing back and forth can shred your nails.

Now start painting! Try to sit still for at least 20 minutes after polishing to make sure your nails are totally dry.

Lola's look

Lola – Colour flash

Flashes of colour can be so much fun. Start by applying a tinted moisturiser with your fingertips, this will provide the perfect canvas to get colour-happy with! Next, eyeliner. Applying doesn't have to be tricky and there are some super-cool coloured ones, my favourite is neon pink – tres cool, which, when worn thickly across your top lashes can look very Audrey Hepburn/punk girl princess.

To ensure minimal eye mess, don't feel like you have to paint one continuous line. Draw three dashes - one at the inner corner, one in the middle of the lash line and another at the outer corner. Then, go back and connect the dashes. For the thick Audrey Hepburn look that I just dig, create your line then start the brush at the middle of your lashes and slowly build up the outer line, extending the liner slightly out and just beyond the eye.

Now sweep a sugar pink blush over the apples of your cheeks before adding a bright colour surge of lip colour to your lips, don't be afraid to clash!

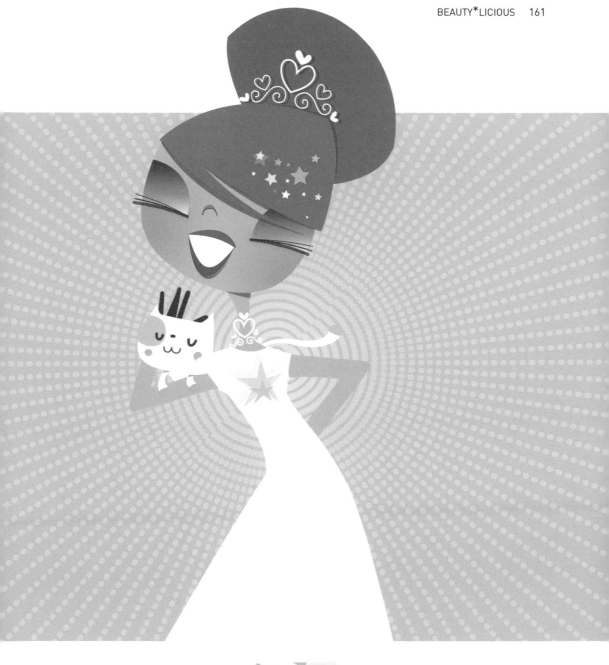

Bella's look

Bella – high octane glam

For movie star flawless skin, you're going to need to use foundation. It should be the same shade as your skin, but if you're in any doubt, use one that's slightly lighter rather than darker. Now, search the house 'til you find the best light available - daylight is always the best option. Sponges are so last year, so instead use your fingers to apply. It warms up your foundation, making it easier to blend. Work on a freshly cleansed and moisturised complexion, give your face cream a minute to sink in, then get blending while your skin still feels plump and moist. This will give you a smooth and slightly slippery surface to work on, and help you get a light, transparent finish.

Now use a dark graphite grey colour over the lid and under the eye to create a smoky effect and finish with lashings of mascara.

For real movie-star glam, a berry red lipgloss will make sure you're on-screen perfection!

Angel's look

Angel – Disco diva

Purple peepers are pure vamp. Purple brings out all natural eye colours, so go as bold as you dare. Cover your entire lid with a pinky-purple shade and blend a dark purple from the middle of the eyelid to the outer edge. Now for the fun bit.

False eyelashes.

By far the coolest accessory I own. False eyelashes can give you an instantly glamorous look and they're easier to apply than you'd imagine. Before you apply the lashes, line your upper lash line with eyeliner and smudge it slightly to create a smoky effect. This will help to conceal the lash band. Lightly pull the lashband through the glue, and wait a moment. Apply the false lashes as close to your natural lash line as possible; press the lash down for a few seconds on the outside of the eye. After you've applied the false lashes, curl them along with your real lashes and apply mascara.

A nude lipgloss will let your eyes do the talking – all you need to do is pout!

Sadie's look

Sadie – Au naturel

Keeping it natural can be just as cool as wearing day-glo brights. Using a tinted moisturiser will even out your skin tone without being as heavy as wearing foundation, but the secret au naturel weapon is blusher. Careful though, because blusher warms with the heat of your body to a more intense hue, which is one reason to apply it very sparingly. Grin into the mirror to see where the apple of your cheek appears. Dip your blusher brush into the powder, shake off the excess, and brush it lightly over the apple of the cheek, moving toward the ear, with short, up-and-down vertical movements. Blend it in with one soft horizontal stroke on top of the vertical strokes, and blot a tissue on top to remove the excess.

To make sure you're ready to glow, finish up with a coat of mascara and a slick of clear gloss.

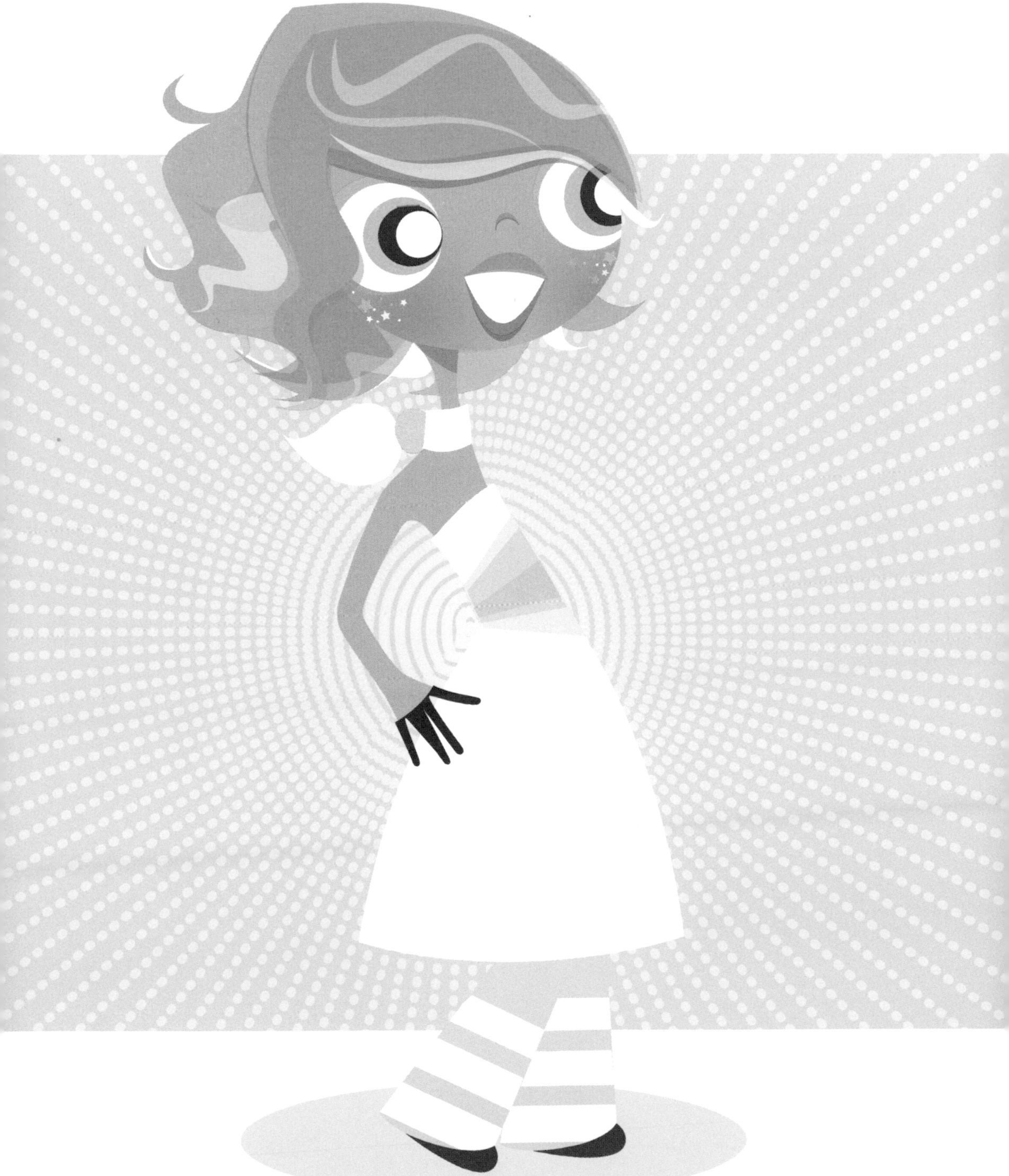

Insider Info

Meet Elke Von Freudenberg. She travels the world as an internationally renowned make-up artist and has the ability to make us feel like Maria in West Side Story – pretty.

Elke - what is it you actually do?
I AM A PHOTOGRAPHY AND CELEBRITY MAKE-UP ARTIST IN LOS ANGELES AND NEW YORK.

What does make-up mean to you?
TO ME, MY IDEA OF MAKE-UP IS WHAT I CALL, 'PRETTY PRETTY'. IT'S DOING BEAUTIFUL MAKE-UP THAT BRINGS OUT THE BEAUTY IN A GIRL, SO THAT YOU SEE THE WHOLE PERSON. NOT JUST HER FACE. IT'S GLOWY, PERFECT SKIN, BEAUTIFUL EYES, GLOSSY LIPS, BLUSH... JUST 'PRETTY PRETTY!' IT'S TAKING YOUR LOOK AND KICKING IT UP A NOTCH. ALL WOMEN WANT TO LOOK 'PRETTY, PRETTY!'

What's your idea of beauty?
TO ME BEAUTY IS FROM THE INSIDE OUT. I CAN DO THE MOST BEAUTIFUL LOOK ON SOMEONE, BUT IF THEY'RE NOT HAPPY, OR ARE RUDE, INCONSIDERATE ETC., ALL OF A SUDDEN, THEY ARE NOT BEAUTIFUL. IT'S DEFINITELY YOUR INNER BEAUTY THAT MAKES YOU BEAUTIFUL.

What would be the must-have items for a Beauty*licious girl's vanity case?

A GREAT MASCARA, A 'FLUSH' BLUSH (A PEACHY PINK), AND A LIPGLOSS. IF THERE IS ONE THING BEAUTY*LICIOUS GIRLS SHOULD KNOW ABOUT THE BEAUTY INDUSTRY IT'S...THE BEAUTY INDUSTRY IS ABOUT WHAT YOU BUY. WE CAN CREATE THE MOST BEAUTIFUL LOOKS, COLOURS ETC, BUT IF YOU DON'T BUY THEM, IT'S GONE! THE CONSUMER REALLY DICTATES WHAT WORKS AND WHAT DOESN'T. IT'S JUST MY JOB TO THROW THEM OUT THERE AND LET YOU PICK!

Tips on how to look feisty, fun, fearless and fabulous the Elke way...

- ★ CONFIDENCE, YOU OWN THE ROOM!
- ★ SMILE.
- ★ BLEND, BLEND, AND BLEND SOME MORE. YOUR MAKE-UP THAT IS, NOT YOUR LOOK!

For regular Beauty*licious beauty tips, check out Elke's Beauty blog:
www.beautynews.blogspot.com

Throw a Sparty!

Tonight, the Glam Girl Squad will be washing our hair, putting on fake lashes, dousing ourselves in our favourite sweet-smelling perfume and watching the entire Marilyn Monroe DVD box set while eating chocolate.

Jealous?

Don't be. Just throw your very own Sparty!

A Sparty is a Glam Girl Squad creation and all you need to throw your own is to combine your favourite Spa-like pampering activities like painting each other's twinkle toes, with party treats like chocolate and DVDs. It really is that simple and is by far the most swanksville way to hang out with your Pink Ladies...

It's your Sparty!

Be a copy kitten and throw your own...

Who will you invite?

....
....
....
....
....
....
....
....
....
....
....

What spa-like activities will you do?

....
....
....
....

....

....

....

....

....

....

What party treats will you provide?

....

....

....

....

....

....

....

....

....

....

....

What will you do? (Our favourites include: dancing to cheesy tunes, having themed DVD-a-thons and singing karaoke)

....

....

....

....

....

....

....

....

....

...gs to do at your *Sparty/Invitation*

The venue
Create a sparty atmosphere by making things comfy with lots of big floor cushions, dim the lights and light some scented candles – sandalwood is my fave.

(Note: Never leave burning candles unattended. That would just be silly.)

Now put on some tunes – think chilled out beats, not rock-girl gee-tars – and cut up slices of fruit to snack on – yum.

Treatment Time
Fresh–faced – Use the DIY Beautista on a Budget products you made earlier to plump up skin, lock in moisture, brighten complexion and, most importantly, to apply to each others faces for the pure laugh-a-bility that seeing your friends look silly will bring.

A Feet treat – mix rock-salt with olive oil and massage onto the soles of each others feet, concentrating on rough areas, then lather on some foot cream to give your tootsies a treat!

Shape up - tidy nails with a nail file, only file in one direction though, and then buff nail beds with a 4-way nail buffer. It will make them stronger, smoother and shinier. Polish off with a cute nail colour. First, use a base coat to fill in any bumpy ridges, then paint on your fave shade and finish with a top coat.

The chill-out zone
Now you're all zen, pampered and feeling fabulous, kick back on the comfy cushions in your dressing gowns, put in a DVD (we'd recommend High School Musical, 13 Going On 30 or if you're feeling retro, Pretty in Pink or Grease) and laugh-out-loud while you recite your favourite lines with your Pink Ladies - bliss. Psst, no one will mind if you occasionally sneak a peek at your newly-painted tootsies, they do look sparkly-gorgeous!

Finishing touches
A Beauty*licious night sleep – getting eight hours shut-eye is the perfect way to end a sparty, not only will it improve your skin tone, it'll help you to remain chilled and relaxed the day after. Ahhhhh.

Sparty!

It's my sparty and you're invited!

who: *Lola Love and the Pink Ladies provide you with everything you need to Spa-aaaaah...*

what: *It's a top-to-toe, at-home, bliss-kissed pampering session to be shared with your very favourite gal pals... Fluffy white salon towels and dressing gowns are not provided, guests must bring their own.*

where: *Your house - because your bathroom is a VIP spa retreat waiting to happen!*

when: *Right now!*

why: *Because pampering is a one-way trip to being truly Beauty *licious!*

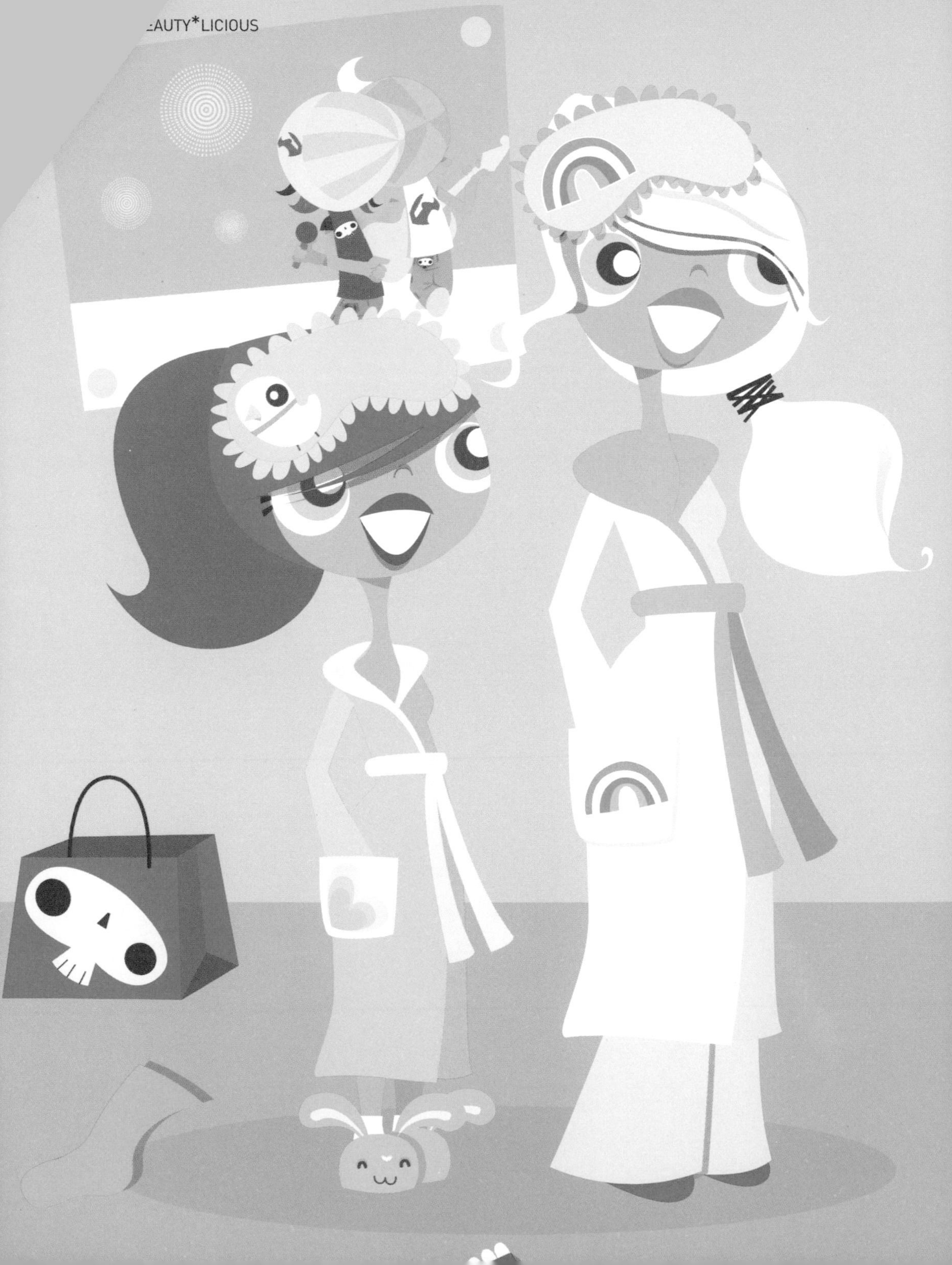

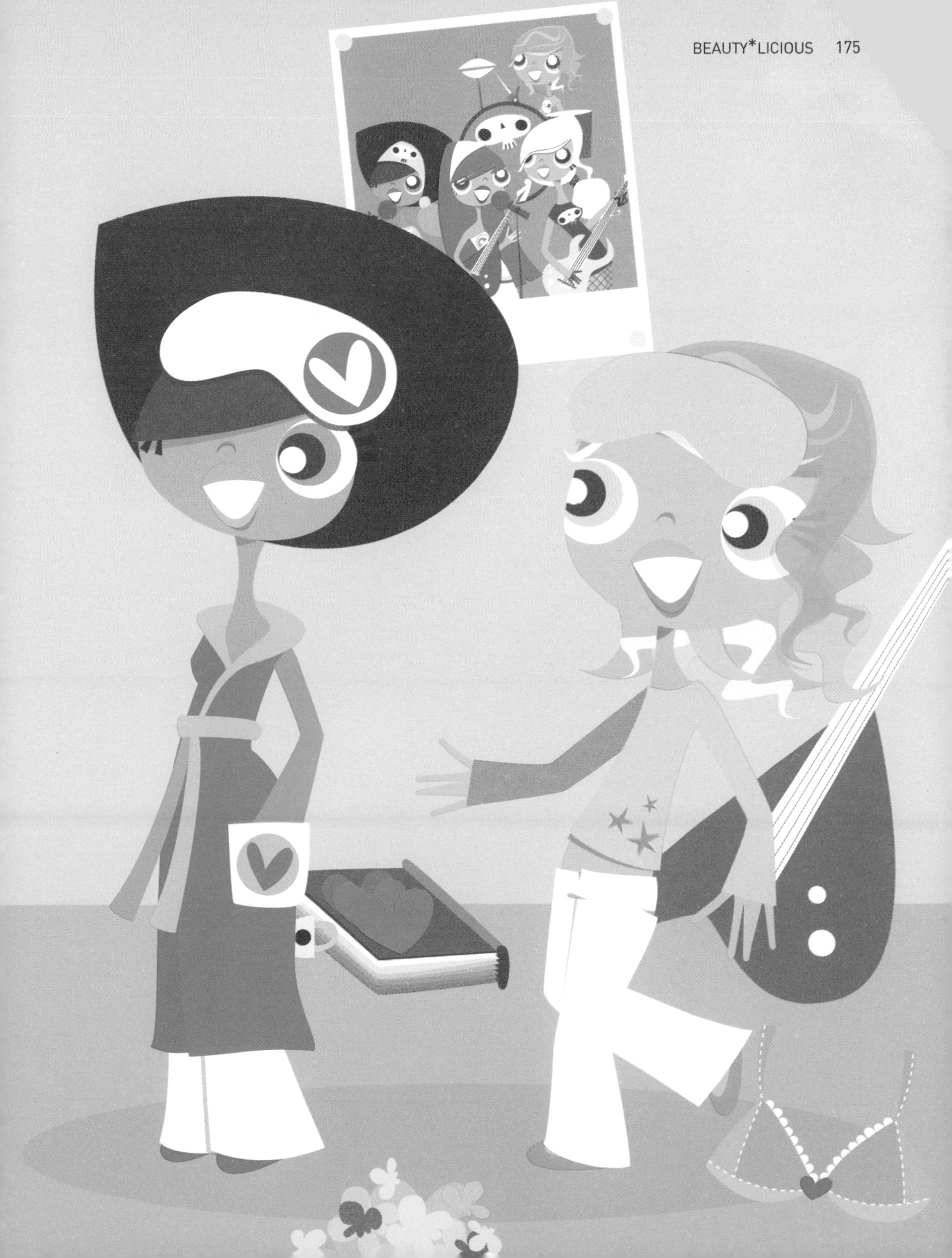

Beauty'licious Parlou

Your ticket to insta-fabdom!

I want cheekbones, is there anything I can do to make me look like I've got them?

THE PINK LADIES: Find a mirror and make a sucked-in-cheek face. See the shadow below your cheekbone? You want to recreate it by sweeping a little bronzer or beige blush right below the bone. Don't overdo it – streaks defeat the whole purpose of sneaky shading. Highlight right above the cheekbone with a pearly shimmer and then apply a smidge of blush to the apples of your cheeks to add a healthy dose of colour. Okay, you can stop pulling the silly face now.

I'm Asian and I never know where to put eye shadow. Help!

THE PINK LADIES: In a nutshell: when you read about shading or brushing eye shadow up to the crease of your lids, don't try to trace the natural fold. Instead use your orbital bone (that's the arc-shaped bone right above your eye socket) as a guide. To sculpt your eyes, start by brushing a pale colour over your entire lid, then blend a deeper shade under the bone and blend it upward. As for your lashes, it's all about eyelash curlers and many, many coats of mascara. Happy experimenting!

What's the best way to wear glitter?

THE PINK LADIES: What's the part of your face that is supposed to sparkle? Answer: you're pretty, pretty eyes, doll-face. Glitter covered eyelids will add a ding-like sound effect every time you blink. Sparkly nail tips and toes rule because, unlike normal polish. You can slap on a couple of coats and your nails will still look totally kawaii. (That's Japanese for cute y'know!)

I'm dark skinned, how do I know what colours to wear?

THE PINK LADIES: Okay, here's your colour cheat sheet. Start by opting for the sheer texture of a tinted moisturiser in a colour close to your skin tone, it will leave your skin feeling lush and let your true fabulous colour shine through. On your cheeks it's best to choose peach shades, anything darker and there's a chance you could look like you're about to overheat. Not good. Try bright, bold colours on both your eyes and lashes. A purple mascara with blue eyeshadow will look hot, hot, hot. Finally, your lips will look fab in anything from pretty pink to deep, dark reds – you lucky thing, you!

Angel trying out her
hot bright makeup combo

Twinkle, twinkle you're a star!

"...You're certified Beauty*licious!..."

Congratulations chica, you are now officially an Academy of all things Beauty*licious graduate - woohoo! You're looking good, feeling great and you now know that the secret to being Beauty*licious isn't all about how you look, it's actually about:

- ✯ Working your YOU-nique qualities like a model-girl whatever your shape or size.
- ✯ Knowing if you don't have it going on inside, looking good on the outside just isn't going to cut it.
- ✯ Putting your body image in perspective – you know how you look is just one small part of the Totally Irreplaceable YOU!

Beauty*licious Girl, you rule!
Love and glitter-pink lip-gloss,

Lola
xx

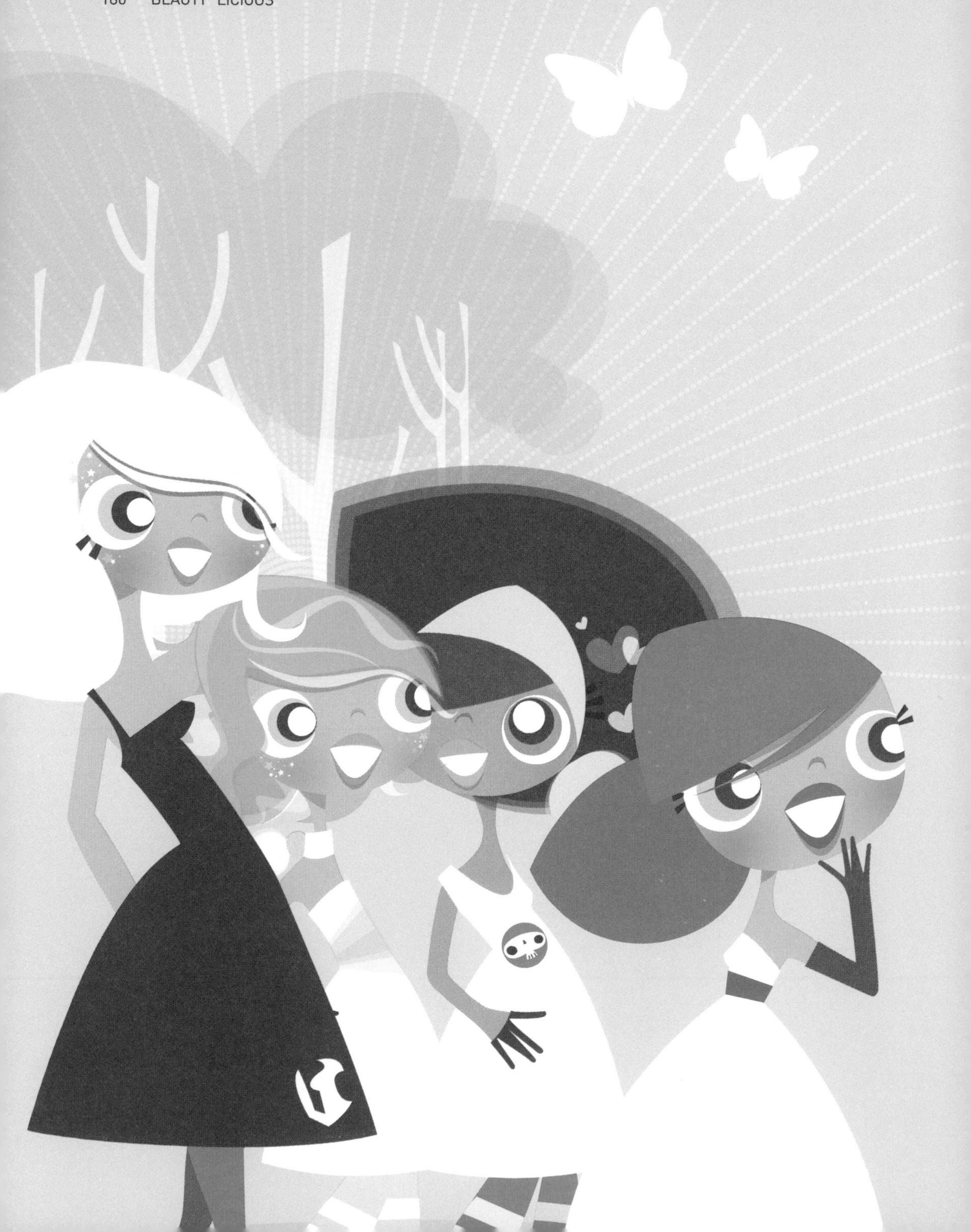

It's official. I, the sparkly-gorgeous

....

(insert your name here)
am totally Beauty*licious!

✭ I don't waste valuable self-lovin' time trashing my looks.

✭ I wear my absolute favourite ensemble to the supermarket – well, why not?

✭ I love my tummy and treat it daily with feel-good food.

✭ I don't make the mistake of letting any kind of trend dictate my YOU-nique style.

✭ I worship at the temple of Me – like, ommmm.

✭ I know that being Beauty*licious is about so much more than just looks. It's about all the amazing things inside and out that make me so super-sparkly that people can't fail to notice me shine!

Signed (your best superstar signature, please!)

....

angel

bella